DOCTOR'S BOY

DOCTOR'S BOY

KARIN ANCKARSVÄRD

Translated from the Swedish by Annabelle MacMillan

ILLUSTRATED BY FERMIN ROCKER

HARCOURT, BRACE & WORLD, INC., NEW YORK

DOCTOR'S BOY

DOCTOR'S BOY

ONE

Jon kicked an apple so hard that it literally flew alongside the gutter. It was a half-rotten, wormy apple, and when the toe of his broad boot hit it, no less than four wasps, buzzing angrily, flew out of it. Jon hopped to one side; just the day before a wasp had stung him in the garden at home. The wasps were lethargic at this time of year but quick to sting.

Jon's eyes searched the hilly cobblestone path to find an apple that looked relatively sound, one that was not already full of wormholes or tooth marks. It was impossible to find one, although several apple trees grew along the way, their strong, gnarled branches stretching far out over the old green rail fence, almost to the street. Come to think of it, it wasn't a bit strange that he couldn't find an apple to eat. A good many children, both from the West Elementary School and the Martell private school went along this cobblestone path, and all of them had eyes as sharp as vultures. The pupils from the West Elementary School in this little Swedish town of Soltuna sometimes even came early in the mornings to be sure of getting their share of the ripe fruit, especially if the previous night had been stormy.

"Oh, well," Jon thought to himself, "I might as well wait

until I get home." Nothing could really compare with their own pears or apples, the latter already overripe as they hung on the laden branches.

He contented himself with a chestnut, which he began to

kick as he trudged on his way. By now he had reached the middle hill. It was the steepest of the three on his way to school, and it was also the most fun.

He could remember clearly how he had stood at the foot of it on his very first day of school, how he had held on to his mother's hand and gazed upward, wondering if he would ever, ever get to the top. Most of all, he had been concerned about his mother, as he looked at her shiny·black shoes that looked so uncomfortable with their high, narrow heels.

Right now he could scarcely imagine that this was the same hill. It was steep, certainly, but it wasn't as perpendicular as it had seemed then, and, besides, the cobblestones were fun to hop along.

Naturally, his mother had accompanied him to school only for a short while—just until she was certain that he could find the way and that he would head over toward the fence if one of the huge brewery wagons happened to come rolling by.

All this had been five years ago. At present he was in the fifth grade and would be eleven next year.

Next year he would no longer need to climb up and down these hills—Three Hill Lane the street was called—but would take off from home in the opposite direction, down the little dead-end street, past the church and the marketplace, all the way to the tall red building with the gold lettering across its façade—the Consolidated Latin School.

Of course, there were examinations to pass before he could go to the Latin School, but these were far from his thoughts at present. To be truthful, he thought about the route to school only when he found himself there, about his textbooks with their printed lines in even rows like soldiers only when they were in front of him, and about the school itself only when he sat at his desk.

In Jon's opinion, school was nothing more than a necessary evil to be endured until the real work of the day began.

The worthwhile work of the world was much more tangible—when the road workers, for instance, laid the even stone paving in front of his father's property, or when Fina and Mari, who helped his mother, did a huge laundry in the washhouse. Work, to Jon, meant helping Soren harness his father's horse Figaro, filling the feed bag with hay and oats, seeing that the blankets and carriage robes were beaten and brushed, and naturally, most important of all, sitting beside his father, who was a doctor, in the gig or sleigh, listening, answering questions, keeping quiet, helping—and all these things at just the right times and in just the right amounts.

Jon hurried along the path in front of his father's house. The windows were a little above his head, but he could see the pale lining of the red drapes in the drawing room, the copper pots filled with plants in the casement windows of the dining room, and a row of jars of lingonberry preserves in the pantry windows. The woods had been filled with lingonberries this autumn, and the open markets had looked very cheerful with huge bins of the red berries on display.

The entrance to the house did not face the street but was around at one side, which gave visitors a feeling of privacy and refinement. To Jon, this gave an additional sense of security. His home wasn't accessible to just anyone. First, you had to open the green gate and walk around one side of the house before you could see the beautiful garden, lush and green, and the wide, inviting porch covered with honeysuckle vines.

During his father's office hours, the gate remained open. But now it was closed. The clock on the church had struck a quarter to four, but even so, Jon was not optimistic that the reception room would be empty. There probably had been a steady stream of patients the whole afternoon because a serious flu epidemic had broken out a week or so ago.

The chill of autumn had already settled on the yellowing garden, and the fogs from the valley to the east rarely cleared now before quite late in the day. Some time ago Soren, the boy from the stoneworks on the other side of the doctor's property, had put the garden furniture away in the tool shed. The lovely season when many of the patients could wait outside in either of the two lilac bowers was a thing of the past.

Now extra chairs had to be placed in the waiting room. The benches along the wall in the hall were crowded with townspeople, truck farmers, women from the stalls in the open markets, and workers from the stone quarry outside of town.

Today it was worse than usual. Standing on tiptoe, Jon peeked through one of the glass panes in the door.

He always wanted to know what awaited him. There were times when it seemed a little creepy to have to walk right through the assembly of waiting patients to get to the door that led to the doctor's private quarters, where he and his father and mother and his brand-new little brother had their own sanctuary remote from the outside world.

Jon couldn't look all the patients in the eye as he passed down the line. He didn't dare. Some of their faces looked quite peculiar—swollen and red or ashen pale or shapeless as potatoes.

The worse part of it was that there was almost always someone he knew among the patients, someone who deserved a special bow—the parents of some of his friends, a clerk from one of the shops, or (and this was even worse) one of the teachers from school.

Jon coped with this problem in his own fashion. He did not take off his cap until he had crossed the threshold, and when he did remove it, he gave it a little swing through the air, which could be interpreted as a greeting to those he knew or a sign of respect to those he didn't, whichever way they wished. Almost all of them knew that he was the doctor's boy. Simultaneously, he cast a hasty glance at one side or other of the assembled crowd. This was almost a routine, but his glance was kindly.

To be on the safe side, however, he always fortified himself for the ordeal by looking through a pane of glass in the door beforehand.

Today it looked pretty bad. Jon noticed their dining-room chairs had been appropriated and placed in the middle between the benches. One, two—six of them. That meant that there were only two left inside, one for Mother and one for him, for their afternoon coffee. The dining room would look strange and empty.

But now he simply had to take the plunge. He pulled the polished brass door handle.

Aha! So they had locked him out. That meant that the nurse had been told not to let any more patients in. There were only so many hours in the day, and his father's house calls were still to come.

The nurse! Suddenly Jon remembered that a new nurse had started to work just today. The previous one had been married during the summer, and for a couple of weeks early in the autumn, Mother herself had helped in the reception room until the new nurse arrived to take over. This had been an unpleasant interlude. Little Brother, only three months old, had taken a dislike to Mari, the maid, and would have no part of her. She had flaming red curly hair, which stood out from her head like a bush. Little Brother noticed the difference between Mari's and Mother's soft, dark wavy hair at once, was frightened, and began to scream.

Thank goodness, that time was over. Mother could return to her own tranquil realm behind the scenes.

Jon had caught just a glimpse of the new nurse as he rushed back to school after lunch. She was tall and thin—bony, in fact—and she had come from one of the big city hospitals. Even that early in the day, she had seemed tense, and on both her cheeks a triangular red spot had appeared.

Somewhat hesitantly now, Jon knocked on the door. He didn't like to have to disturb the nurse; she might be doing something important for Father at that very moment. There was a back entrance to the house, of course, but the family never used it. Furthermore, to get to it, he would have to go out on the street again and walk halfway around the house.

Once again Jon knocked, this time harder and more purposefully. A few of the patients stirred restlessly, and an old lady in a black shawl, who was sitting close to the door, made a motion as if she wanted to get up and open the door but didn't dare to.

At that moment the new nurse dashed to the door. The old lady settled in her seat once more, seemingly glad that she hadn't exerted herself unnecessarily, and the door opened out so suddenly that it almost hit Jon in the face.

"Office hours were over a long time ago. The doctor can't receive any more patients today!"

13

With great determination the nurse jerked the door toward her, almost managing to shut it again, but Jon was quick on his feet, even when unexpected things happened. He managed to plant his heavy boot in the doorway, and he grabbed the door handle.

"Well, I'm coming in anyway," he said emphatically. "I live here."

Noticing the indignant expression that appeared on her long face, he added with a slight twitch at the corners of his mouth, "I'm the doctor's boy!"

Bewildered, the nurse stepped aside. A few of the patients murmured their comments, and some of the men— ice wagon or van drivers, judging from their leather aprons —laughed.

Jon did not wish to confuse the nurse any more than necessary, so he fastened his gaze on the old lady in the black shawl. She was a true lady and wouldn't dream of laughing out loud, but her shoulders shook slightly beneath her shawl.

Jon tipped his cap to the nurse. She might be completely impossible, but it would never do to irritate her. There was a shortage of nurses in that part of the country, and Jon remembered that his mother needed to be free to take care of Little Brother.

"Good afternoon," he said.

Being unable to think of anything more to say, he stepped across the threshold and hurried past the interested glances of the patients.

A little while later, Jon and Mother sat facing one another in the dining room enjoying their coffee. That is to

say, Jon drank hot chocolate, but the ritual was always referred to as "afternoon coffee."

Mother sat on the one remaining dining-room chair, since the nurse had rushed in just as they were about to be seated and taken the other one. Mother had nodded amiably because she was accustomed to having the household chairs wander out to the reception room, but the nurse's expression had been forbidding. Clearly, she felt that the doctor should certainly not have asked her to admit that insistent latecomer. As a matter of fact, he should have called a halt to the stream of patients much earlier than he had.

When the reception room was full, it was full. That was the way it had been at the hospital where she had worked, and that was all there was to it! If you received all the ailing and unfortunate people who happened along, your working day would never come to an end.

To use the doctor's private house for an infirmary didn't seem orderly or right to her. She thought it low class. There ought to be a clear-cut line between the doctor, his assistants, and his family on the one side—after all, they were educated people—and the masses in the reception room on the other. The nurse was far from sure that this was so in the doctor's house, and for that reason she shrugged her shoulders as she asked the doctor's wife if she could have still another chair.

The last patients to arrive should just stand and wait to her way of thinking, but the doctor had stuck his head out from the office, surveyed his battlefield, and ordered her to bring in the dining-room chairs. They were elegant chairs, too, with leather cushions and carved backs.

Mother and Jon had been aware of the nurse's annoyance, and they looked at one another over their cups, not without some concern. Jon was sitting on a stool that was usually kept by the sewing table near the dormer window. He was perfectly happy with the arrangement; he was fond of the three-cornered stool with its lathe-turned legs and embroidered cushion.

Mother and Jon shared the kind of understanding that relies very little on spoken words or explanations.

"She was so happy with her room," Mother said with a little sigh, "but it's a shame that this flu epidemic had to hit just before her arrival."

"Well, the epidemic isn't as bad as last year yet," Jon remarked. "Remember when Father didn't get any sleep for three whole days?"

"I doubt that things will reach that stage this year. . . . Of course, this nurse comes to us from a hospital, where visiting hours were strictly kept, as they had to be. But here things are different," Mother said as she broke off a piece of one of Mari's soft gingersnaps. "But we've got to be careful with her. You know, Jon, how hard it is to get anyone to work in this part of the world. And she does seem clean and efficient and capable."

Jon nodded. His brain was hard at work. He was a healthy-looking, attractive boy with a shock of unruly hair falling across his forehead.

"I can't see that she has much to fuss about," he said as he wiped a chocolate mustache from his upper lip. "When office hours are over, she's free. Do you know, by the way, if there are many house calls to make today?"

Mother looked a little troubled.

"By one o'clock there were already three," she said as she

traced the lines of the embroidery on the tablecloth with her finger. "And Father said they were all important. Old lady Larsson out at the poorhouse. She's ninety-three, you know, and she's always been in good health. Even if she has nothing more than a touch of flu now, it could be serious because of her age. Naturally, your father can't disappoint her."

Mother looked out of the window. An enormous open dray, loaded with gravestones fresh from the stoneworks and drawn by two powerful work horses, rumbled down the hill.

Perhaps it occurred to her that her son's world was colored by a good deal of talk about sickness and death. She tried to change the subject to something more appropriate.

"How did school go today?"

Jon's eyebrows shot up. They were dark, narrow, and nicely arched—the one somewhat mature feature about a face that otherwise was round and soft. He was not particularly pleased to be reminded of school. It was always hard for him to remember trivial things, but for Mother's sake he tried.

"Oh, well, we had math and music. I can't sing for sour apples, the teacher says. Elsa knocked over the inkwell again today, and the teacher really got mad. But Elsa's eyes are bad. Mother, do you think there's any medical cure for someone who's cross-eyed?"

There—they were back on *important* subjects again, and Jon had accomplished this so skillfully that Mother didn't even notice until she was well into a description of all she knew about crossed eyes—information she had gleaned from Father.

18

She interrupted herself suddenly when she realized she had fallen into a trap.

"Jon, what do you do at recess? Do you have a good time? What games do you play?"

"Well," Jon began nonchalantly, "I have a good time. We had a sack race today. Rickard won—he always does. I came in fourth."

Jon sounded as if he were miles away. Mother watched him with humorous anxiety. She desperately wanted him to be like other children, rushing around, playing wildly, falling down and hurting his knees—even getting a few demerits in conduct on his report card, which had to be signed every Sunday and returned to the teacher every Monday morning.

But then she recalled Father's comments on the subject. " 'Like other children.' What other children? Every child is different from every other. We don't demand of ourselves that we be 'like other grownups,' because we know that human beings run the gamut from giants to dwarfs, from saints and geniuses to killers and idiots."

It was evident now that Jon was in a great hurry to finish his sweet roll, to drink the last drops of hot chocolate. She sighed as he jumped to his feet as if he had been attacked by a swarm of bees, hugged her, and gave her a quick kiss. Grabbing his schoolbag, he hurried straight to his room, where she knew he would set a new time record for doing his homework.

She felt that there was something slightly apologetic about his kiss. It was that way with Father's, too, when he was about to leave on his house visits.

"Forgive me, my dear," he'd say, "but I have such a tremendous load of work to do, things that can't be put off. There is need all around us—the sick, the crippled, the unfortunate. I know you wouldn't have me neglect them— otherwise you wouldn't be you. Actually, I don't really need to beg your forgiveness . . ."

No. Mother gazed out at the fast-approaching autumn twilight, sensing that it had grown quite chilly. This made her think of storm windows and weather stripping. Soon she would have to buy some artificial flowers to decorate the place a bit—and then, almost before you could turn around, it would be time to replace the artificial flowers with Christmas stars, gold ornaments, and red woolen elves.

A weak but insistent cry from another part of the house brought her back down to earth. Little Brother had awakened.

She lifted up her long flounced skirt as if suggesting to herself that she had better hurry. Her thoughts turned to piles of baby clothes, safety pins, and lace-trimmed baby caps.

TWO

"The poorhouse, Quarry Road, and one of the cottages on Helge Ridge," Father said tersely, and by the tone of his voice you knew that these three places were not three addresses in his mind but particular ailments, people in beds, on sofas, or, as could happen, on mattresses or cushions right on the floor.

Jon was pretty well aware of what various homes looked like, because when there was no risk of infection and an illness was not too serious, he was allowed to go in with his father. It always cheered the old ladies at the poorhouse to have a youngster visiting them; and children who had just suffered a bad stomach upset—"Green apples? Oh, I see! Plums. Well, they are plump and lovely this year!" Father would say—quickly calmed down when the doctor, whom they had dreaded, was preceded by a thin boy they recognized from having seen him on the street or at school. They would tell Jon in detail about the suffering they had undergone, while the doctor and the relieved parents retired to an adjoining room to discuss a suitable diet for the young patient.

Of course, at times there was no "adjoining room." Instead, the sick person shared a room with the rest of the family, perhaps the only one with a stove, which meant that the room smelled strongly of food and was often terribly warm.

Jon was not surprised by seeing things of this sort. Several of his classmates lived in this type of home; they were scholarship students, and they were sometimes amazingly diligent and bright in a good many subjects.

The list of calls for the day didn't sound too promising, and since the flu was rather widespread, Jon was sure he would have to stay outside and keep Figaro company instead of going in to visit the sick.

The gig joggled and swayed as they rolled out through the gate. Both wheels were equipped with massive rubber tires, and the gig, newly lacquered in black and gold, had a simple spring base. It was the general opinion that the doctor and his boy traveled in a highly modern and comfortable vehicle.

This evening the carriage apron of fur-lined velvet was in use for the first time that season, and Father fastened it carefully around their legs before he took the reins.

Figaro pricked up his ears and snorted. The frosty chill in the air, a handful of oats before starting, and the promise of a regal evening meal when they returned home had instilled in this well-cared-for, healthy animal the feeling that life was a delight and a joy, well worth participating in.

As usual, Father seemed a bit preoccupied, but also, as usual, he noticed much more than you would have believed. "Where is your scarf, Jon?"

Jon put his hand to his coat collar. Mentally, he retraced

the events of the day. This morning? Yes, this morning Mother had put it around his neck.

"It's at school," he answered discreetly. "Yes, it must be. On the shelf. I remember distinctly that I put it right beside my cap, but then I put just the cap on and forgot the scarf."

"If you'd just put it in your coat sleeve," Father remarked, "then you'd always have it where you couldn't forget it, wouldn't you? Your throat is altogether too exposed."

"I tried that once," Jon said. "But the kids bump against the coats in the hall, and sometimes when they're trying to avoid some teacher, they hide there, and then the scarf falls on the floor. And you can't imagine, Father, what a scarf looks like then, especially with the weather we've been having. Mud and slush all over the place."

At Main Street, which ran parallel to the river, they turned. On the one side were some fairly new municipal buildings several stories high, built of stone, and here the poultry dealers, bakers, clothiers, and hardware merchants had their shops. Enameled sheet-metal signs clanked and creaked from the poles on which they were suspended. One particularly elegant-looking shop had a black glass sign on either side of the door. The gold lettering stated that Wines, Spirits, and Antiques were for sale inside.

On the other side of the street were one-family frame houses with balconies and glass-enclosed verandas, painted red, green, yellow, or white. Some of them boasted small bathhouses down near the river's edge, and all of them were surrounded by lovely gardens and rail or picket fences.

Jon could see only the white houses now; the others were concealed by the darkness that was increasing with every passing moment.

The gig rolled along softly and quietly, thanks to the rubber tires and a blanket of leaves that the wind had blown from the gardens but that had been halted in its course by the walls on the other side.

"Scarves are not very practical," said Father, who had a talent for dealing with a problem exhaustively. "You'd be much better off with a high collar on your coat. Even better, a fur collar like the one I have on my driving coat. I want you to ask Mother if she will take your winter coat down to Jensson's and have them sew a fur collar on it. They can use cat's fur or lamb's wool, but you should be able to button it way up around your throat."

Jon sat quietly. He was trying to imagine what his coat —and he himself, for that matter—would look like with a fur collar. He could picture striped cat's fur or curly white sheepskin.

He tried to recall if he had ever seen a boy's coat with a fur collar. He was quite sure he never had.

"No other boy in school has a coat with a fur collar. The girls have them sometimes—the ones who can afford it— but just the girls," Jon said hesitantly.

"No other boy in school rides around for miles in rain and snow and sleet and wind as you do," Father reminded him.

Jon began to have second thoughts. What Father said was true. He recalled how uncomfortable it was when the snowflakes began to collect around his neck. To be sure, the gig had a top, which could be put up, but that was no protection against the cold, and none at all against rain and snow if you were facing into the wind. Several times the previous winter he had had a sore throat, and toward spring he had contracted a stubborn cough, which had kept him inside the house.

No doubt Father was right. His throat should be protected. He would certainly be conspicuous among his classmates, but which was more important—to look just like everybody else or to be allowed to go with his father on his rounds of house calls?

There was only one answer to that question. If it would keep him in good health, Jon would willingly have submitted to wearing monkey fur around his throat.

"I'll speak to Mother," he said.

Nodding, Father lapsed into his former silence. He was seldom very talkative until they were on the way home. If he were silent then, this meant that he had his doubts about the outcome of some particular illness and was pondering over it. Without actually being aware of how he knew, Jon was always able to tell when Father was disturbed about something and needed to be left in peace and quiet.

Jon began to think about the call Father had to make this evening on Quarry Road. There were really two Quarry Roads—each very distinctive—although the one, quite naturally, was no more than a continuation of the other. There was the part that was inside the city limits and the part out in the country, which stretched for miles. If you had to go to the part out in the country, this meant quite a long journey, because for a considerable stretch there were no buildings at all. The road wound across barren hills, between uneven mossy stone walls that had been built when the land was cleared and through scrubby pine forests. Eventually, you would come upon a couple of gray cottages, followed by rows of long barracks where the workers lived. And that brought you up to the colossal shaft of the quarry, which, even in the darkness, seemed a good deal blacker than its surroundings.

"Luckily," Father said as if he had been reading Jon's mind, "we're not going out to the quarry. There's not much light left in that candle."

Jon peered at the flame that burned in the carriage lantern at his elbow. Mentally, he measured the height of the candle. Not much, but it would do!

He felt a small tingle of excitement. On the part of Quarry Road that was within the city limits, there was only one building that was inhabited. The rest of the buildings were sheds, dilapidated stables where the truck farmers kept their horses in the winter, and storerooms for junk.

Father drove first to the poorhouse.

"Old lady Larsson is probably waiting for me," he said with a chuckle. His gleaming white teeth were in sharp contrast to his short, clipped black beard.

Jon chortled too. He remembered old lady Larsson from an earlier visit. She had looked very odd—toothless, mustached, with tufts of hair sticking straight out from her ears. Then he recalled the special sort of gentleness with which Father treated his patients. Father liked them. Just by a small laugh, he managed to make them feel that they were one big, happy family or, perhaps more rightly, part of a brotherhood where sickness and fragility, even moral lapses and other defects, were the cards of admission.

Old lady Larsson had the reputation of being excessively quarrelsome, but Father spoke of this failing of hers in such a gentle, joking manner that Jon himself, to say nothing of the personnel at the poorhouse, came to regard it as a sign of senility that could happen to anyone and that shouldn't be taken too seriously. There were times when he would give the old lady quite an argument, which she clearly enjoyed so much that she finally dissolved in paroxysms of laughter.

"It would be a shame if this flu epidemic were to be the

end of her," Father said, handing Jon the reins before he climbed down out of the gig, carrying his brown leather case in one hand. "She's ninety-three—our oldest citizen—and she's still enjoying life."

Jon watched his tall, thin, somewhat bent figure disappear between the yellow cottages. The poorhouse consisted of not just one building but of several cottages built around a pretty little park. Lights shone from the various windows, but the street, where Jon and Figaro were left alone, was deep in darkness. The nearest street lantern, only recently lit by the lamplighter, was down at the corner of Main Street and illuminated only a very limited area.

But Jon was not afraid. He was used to waiting in dark streets, and Figaro was good company. At the beginning Mother had expressed certain doubts about Jon's being allowed to accompany his father on his rounds, but Jon had pleaded and cajoled. He was no more than eight when he began to feel that it was not worth his while to stay home with Mother and Mari, where it was warm and light, while Father was out on his important calls. And it had not been difficult to persuade Father. He liked company, believed that a boy should not lead too sheltered a life, and was not in the least worried.

There were discussions about the risk of infection and "disreputable drunks," but Father assured her that Jon would not be allowed to come near contagious diseases, even though his own father was always risking infection and contagion, and as to "disreputable drunks," Jon would sooner or later bump into them anyway. In the gig he was quite protected, and if worse came to worst, he could always drive away with Figaro. Moreover, it was just as well if there were someone to look after Figaro.

Thus it was that Father, Jon, and Figaro had become a little corporation, and the people of Soltuna had grown accustomed to seeing the doctor's gig on the streets with both passengers, the one quite tall and the other quite small. They would notice the gig on lovely spring evenings— elegant with its soft, well-plumped cushions and the frisky, shiny, well-groomed Figaro—but they knew that it was out, too, in the autumn rain and the winter snow, on evenings when they could make out no more detail than the glimmer of a lantern and the fact that it was a one-horse carriage rolling by.

Something of stability and security lay in all this, although comments would often be tinged with anxiety:

"I wonder what's going on over at the Nilssons. The doctor's gig is outside their house."

Or, "Did you notice that the doctor drove along Vidinge Road yesterday evening? I wonder if the old man is sick again."

When it was light, time and time again Father would have to tip his hat to the right and to the left, and Jon would have to remove his cap with the little star insignia that meant that he was a pupil at the Martell School.

The house call on old lady Larsson didn't last very long.

"She's not in any danger," Father said, taking the reins and signaling Figaro on. "She has a nasty cough, but it will get better with the stronger medicine I prescribed for her. She'll have a calm night. Nothing wrong with her lungs."

They drove around the poorhouse, and soon they were

bobbing up and down on the deserted, uninhabited section of Quarry Road.

"These cobblestones are bone-shakers," Father said disapprovingly. "It's a good thing we have rubber tires."

The candle flame fluttered inside the glass covering of the carriage lantern.

They stopped in front of the one inhabited building on this part of Quarry Road—a notorious one it was, too. The entry consisted of a stone gateway with an arched roof, which led to a long, dim courtyard that was dark even in the daytime. Leading from both the archway and the courtyard were stairways that were dark and that smelled of cabbage.

One time Jon had had to run down to the apothecary shop and get a thermometer for one of the patients in the building. Father had come outside and sent him on the errand.

"Nobody here has one, and they'll never have sense enough to get one, either. And I've got to know this evening whether the temperature has gone up or not. I'd like to keep my own thermometer."

Father had given Jon some money, and when he returned, he had had to climb up one of the narrow stairways with its gray worn steps. Half-grown boys had been standing there, leaning against the archway. Jon had felt his heart beating wildly. But they had made room for him and said nothing except to ask what the horse's name was.

Jon recalled the strange smells, mainly cabbage. The patient was a child, and it had seemed to Jon that no adult was to be found anywhere near the child. Later on he heard that Father had had to send for a social worker to watch over the child.

30

Jon sat very quietly in his place. The reins rested across his lap. Figaro, as well, kept motionless. Father had spread a fine, heavy checkered blanket across Figaro's back before going inside, because by that time the horse had grown warm, and he might easily get chilled in the frosty evening temperature.

Both Jon and Figaro felt that it was best to call as little attention to themselves as possible. In the archway, lighted by a solitary gas light suspended from an iron frame, could be seen glimpses of various figures. Shouts and laughter could be heard in the long, narrow courtyard. Yellowish lights shone from a few of the windows, some of which were open.

Something was moving in the darkness some distance down the street. Was it only the shadows of the elms over that way or was someone approaching? Shadows fell to and fro across the muddy footpath.

No, it wasn't the shadows of the elms. It was a fellow who was staggering. Suddenly and unexpectedly, he bellowed, fell against the wall, and remained there swaying for a couple of minutes before he could regain his balance. Then he resumed his wobbly path toward the archway.

Just as he reached a cellar stairway, which led down several steps below street level, a window on the third floor was thrown open. The yellowish light up there grew stronger, and an indescribable medley of shouting voices, banging and thumping, china smashing, and the asthmatic tones of a hand organ could be heard clear down on Quarry Road.

Something came sailing out of the open window and fell to the ground right in front of the swaying figure. The

empty whisky bottle broke as it hit a gravel pile, which, in the midst of all the mud, had managed to withstand the ravages of the late summer rains.

The fellow took a couple of shaky steps to one side, steps that were entirely too unsteady. He fell down the cellar stairway.

Figaro's nerves had been on edge ever since the window had opened. Jon held the reins tightly and muttered, "There, there, boy," a number of times after the bottle broke. Then he sat completely motionless and quiet. He had heard that drunken people could be highly unpredictable, could become angry suddenly and direct their rage at innocent bystanders. As yet, however, he didn't feel this situation was serious enough to warrant his driving away with Figaro.

He began to wonder what might have happened had the bottle fallen a split second later. Could the man have survived a direct hit from the third story? The greater the distance a falling object had to travel, the greater the force, Jon knew.

He peered at the area near the cellar stairway. Figaro also turned his head. He was always on the alert when human beings approached him and, strangely enough, even more so when these humans behaved peculiarly or looked suspicious. His sensitive nostrils had already picked up the scent of alcohol, and this he didn't like. Anytime an amiable, well-meaning drunk approached him with the idea of petting him, he recoiled. Figaro was very wise, Father said.

Sure enough, the man was crawling out of the cellarway. A puddle of muddy water had collected in a little hollow above the cellar stairway. He crawled straight through it. He certainly was drunk, Jon mused.

In his thick-tongued fashion, the man swore terribly once he managed to get to his feet. He wavered as he passed the doctor's gig. Staring in Jon's direction, he shouted something. Jon made himself as insignificant as possible. He was pretty sure the man's foggy eyes couldn't see him tucked away in his corner. In any case, he was glad that Figaro hadn't had to face this encounter all by himself.

The fellow disappeared down the archway. Inside, there was a great deal of renewed commotion as he passed by. Jon began to peer in that direction, as did Figaro. Not that you could see much with the inadequate lighting, but they could hear that the fellow was the object of a good deal of laughter and derision. The commotion, however, was short-lived. An unsteady drunk was certainly no sensation in that building on Quarry Road.

Jon wished vaguely that he could get a closer look at the dirty archway and the dimly lighted courtyard. How could babies and children live in a place like that? The adults referred to it as a "haunt," shook their heads, and called the police or other authorities. Now and then, of course, the police—always in pairs—with their long, dangling sabers, would patrol that section of the road.

But Jon was puzzled. What *could* boys—you never saw many girls—who were just a few years older than he find to do in this place, which, if outward appearance meant anything, was both dangerous and criminal? There was a good deal going on in the world of which he had no notion.

Did they sit around getting drunk? If so, how could they afford it? Father referred to them as poor, destitute creatures. Did they spend their time fighting? Yes, that was a fairly safe conclusion. But they could hardly carry on like that night after night.

Was it possible they were receivers of stolen goods? Did they attack passers-by and rob them of watches and wallets? But how could they get away with that, right in the middle of town? The police station and the lockup were no more than five minutes away.

What was it Mother so often said as she gazed out at the autumn darkness when everything seemed so gray?

"You know," she would say, "we should count our blessings more often. We don't realize how good things are for us!"

Then she would laugh, of course. It was easy to get Mother to laugh. And she would kiss Jon or Father or Little Brother—whoever happened to be around.

But perhaps there were people who had no one to kiss or who had never been kissed at all.

Jon shivered. Figaro, beginning to be restless over the long wait, shook himself so hard that his harness rattled.

THREE

Just at that point, something moved right beside the gig. Jon jumped a foot. He hadn't seen anything approaching from the rear. The night was coal black except for the small circle of illumination from the gig's lantern.

"Hey, you," a hoarse feminine voice said, almost in a whisper, "you're the doc's boy, ain't ya?"

Jon looked down at the speaker, who was by now standing in the circle of light. It was a girl about his own age, coatless, but wearing a heavy sweater that reached below her hips and a dark shapeless skirt that seemed too big for her slight figure. The collar of the sweater, which looked very much like a boy's garment, was fastened around her throat with a strap.

"And if you're the doc's boy," she continued, "then you oughta know somethin'—what happens when people have babies. It's the same with animals, ain't it? Pixie"—and here the girl's voice almost disappeared, but she managed with much effort to continue speaking—"Pixie, she's in there, and I don't think she's gonna make it. Come on down!" she suddenly screamed in a shrill voice. "Whatsa matter with your ears, boy? Shake a leg!"

Jon didn't understand what she was talking about—except that she wanted him for something. She began jerking at the carriage rug and, realizing that it was fastened, tried to get it loose. Jon cast a dubious glance at Figaro.

"You can leave the horse, can't you? Sure you can! Nothin' wrong with the horse! Come, I said."

Jon climbed down. He wanted to ask a question, but she gave him no chance. She hurried toward the archway with Jon following behind her, half motivated by curiosity, half acting against his better judgment.

The inside of the archway was broader than he had remembered. The walls lay in complete darkness. The entrances to the various stairways were closed because of the penetrating cold. A couple of men stood beside one of the entranceways, but otherwise the area was empty of people.

The girl rushed straight through the archway and out into the adjacent courtyard. The middle part of this was elevated and seemed to be the roof over some sort of cellar area below. She ran around to the side. Over toward the largest of the entrances was a gas light, but this was the only illumination in the courtyard. In the flickering light, Jon noticed garbage cans full to overflowing and a couple of barrels.

A rough wall closed in the courtyard at one end. If you looked high enough, you could see a small piece of the night sky, but on this particular evening there were no stars, no moon. Next to the wall was a feeble attempt at a flower bed—at least there was some loose dirt and a few broken flower stalks of uncertain origin.

A group—mostly of children and young people, if you were to judge by height and weight—was assembled over there. No doubt they were the ones who had been making so much noise at the street entrance.

Without any special interest, they moved aside to let the girl through; Jon was right at her heels. She obviously belonged there and was a part of whatever was taking place in that corner of the world.

Over in the corner by the wall lay a small dog stretched out on a piece of dirty blanket. Its legs were short, but it was somewhat larger than a dachshund. It was black and smooth-haired, with some light spots, either yellow or white, on its chest and on both front feet. Ever afterwards a vivid picture of the dog as it lay there, motionless but seemingly not dead, would linger in Jon's mind.

"I found 'er a half hour ago," said the girl, who had dropped to her knees near the dog's head and begun to pet it. "She disappeared yesterday mornin'. I brought the blanket out here and made 'er lie down. Two are dead as doornails, and they look terrible, but two of 'em are warm, and one breathed just a little while ago. It'd be swell if we could keep 'em alive, wouldn't it?"

Jon, who realized that this must be the "Pixie" to whom the girl had referred, now became aware of the other objects on the blanket—two small blobs that one of the nearby observers had pointed out with his foot by way of explanation. Another lay right in front of Jon, and finally there was the one pressed up close to the dog's nose.

"I put it there so she'd begin to lick it. She did that when the others came—the dead ones—but now it seems she hasn't the strength to go on. D'ya think there are gonna be more? She'll never pull through if there are."

The girl sounded worried and, at the same time, officious.

Obviously, she felt she had handled the whole situation pretty well.

Jon felt as if he were paralyzed, both by her absolute trust and by the curiosity of the group standing around. He realized that the dog had had puppies, but he had never seen anything like this in his life. The only birth that had ever touched him closely had been that of Little Brother, whom he had seen for the first time after he had been dressed, so that only his little red face and tufts of black hair were visible. But the event had taken place at home. Mrs. Lundgren, the midwife, and another practical nurse had been summoned in great haste, and in the kitchen they had boiled so much water that the cast-iron stove glowed red. Even to this day, Jon had wondered how a creature as tiny as Little Brother could have needed so many kettles of boiling water. It wasn't surprising that he looked like a cooked lobster when he was finally put on display.

Jon crouched down at the girl's side. Quickly removing his woolen mittens, he reached out and cautiously touched the little black lump that lay close to the dog's nose. He very nearly jumped—it felt slippery and slimy, not at all as he had expected. He had always thought of a puppy as something warm and soft.

The many pairs of eyes that were focused on him gave him strength. He finally got a good grip on the little black, wet blob. He was quite sure that it felt warm. At the end of its thin neck dangled its little head. This didn't look too promising, but he caught sight of the puppy's face, and his confidence began to rise. It looked very wrinkled and somehow ridiculous, but there was no doubt it was a dog's face in miniature. The eyes were nothing more than two wrinkles among all the other wrinkles, but it had a nose and a little red tongue, a real forehead with a white spot on it, and tiny ears.

Jon groped about, pressing the spot where he thought the heart ought to be, and he was pretty sure that he could feel a weak "thump-thump." On a sudden hunch—he decided that it would be a good thing to get the puppy's mouth open—he carefully pulled at the end of the little tongue.

It turned out to be a good move. As the puppy opened its unexpectedly large mouth and yawned in an almost blasé fashion, white foam trickled down at the corners. Jon took a handkerchief from his pocket and wiped the foam away. He wiped the inside of its mouth a little, too, and now all of them could see the chest heaving and the paws, no bigger than pennies, beginning to move.

This miracle relieved the general tension, and a whole chorus of voices began to make themselves heard.

"Hey, how about that!"

"The character's alive!"

"Hey, he's real cute, ain't he?"

The girl said, "Didn' I tell ya? Didn' I tell ya! Just imagine. Maybe we can keep both of 'em alive!"

"Boy, that'd make your mother real happy, as crowded as you are up there!" A hoarse adolescent laugh followed that comment, which, strange to say, didn't receive much support from the others.

Another voice said, "Somebody always has to give a bunch of advice!"

The girl couldn't care less about the opinions of the others. She stared seriously at Jon, who, encouraged by his success thus far, was using his handkerchief to rub the

patient dry. He had enough sense to realize that the puppy ought to be dry and warm as quickly as possible. For the first time, he felt the lack of his long wool scarf.

"Hey! Maybe you can work on this one, too. It breathed just a little while ago; I swear it did!"

Jon was crouched on his heels. The girl placed the other puppy on his knee. This one was black, but there was a little white spot on its tail.

By now Jon was so self-confident that he began to let his voice be heard. "I could use some warm water. This one feels so limp," he said. "And something to wrap around it. I'm afraid it's going to freeze to death otherwise. It's terribly cold out here. Cold as the dickens!"

The assembled group maintained a respectful silence. The girl turned to one of the group who was closest.

"Shake a leg, Ricky, and get 'im what he wants. But *warm* water . . . well, it's possible that Maw has something on the stove."

"But listen!" she screamed at the disappearing figure. "Don't you say a word about Pixie. Say that I fell down and skinned my knee and that I gotta wash off the blood!"

As they waited, a pleasanter atmosphere seemed to spring up around the dog and the puppies. Everyone felt happier when the star of the drama, the brand-new mother, rather unexpectedly sat up and forcefully and energetically began to lick first herself and then her two little ones.

"She's not gonna bother with the two dead ones," someone remarked.

"It's obvious to her that they're dead," another suggested.

Little by little, it occurred to the onlookers that the whole

42

thing had been rather natural and that Jon's methods had been very simple—things that anybody could have done, and suddenly they, too, were full of good advice.

"You oughta get 'er some warm milk!"

"And somethin' to eat!"

"And you oughta give 'er a bath. You should take and carry 'er up to your kitchen!"

The latter remark caused the girl to look very perplexed. "That'd be the worstest thing in the world!" she ventured. "I can't just leave her lay here, and I don't dare take 'er upstairs. What would Maw say? She practically wouldn't lemme have Pixie."

From the back row, someone suddenly said scoffingly, "Hey, look there. Here comes somebody who knows what goes on!"

Jon turned around. Along the grayish yellow wall flew a shadow of almost terrifying proportions, moving at great speed, almost as if it were in flight.

To his astonishment, in a second Jon recognized it. He had seen the same shadow crossing the doctor's nicely raked path and lovely lawn in the July twilight the night that Little Brother was born. It had been spooky that time as well.

His eyes followed the passing figure. The woman was bent. She had on a Spanish cloak and a black hat. For a brief moment, he wondered if she truly was coming to help Pixie . . . but a minute later, she had disappeared up one of the entranceways leading to the houses facing the court-yard.

A murmur arose from the assembled group. The hoarse feminine voice was heard again.

"Mrs. Lundgren! The midwife! Don't you see—she's on her way to the Svenssons! And there goes this kid's old man, too!"

"You should call him the doctor," came the voice of another, who clearly had some sense of propriety.

"Well, it's his old man, anyway, you dope!"

"Yeah, but we don't have to pay any respect to the boy. He's just a boy!"

Jon, having risen to his feet, stood with his mouth agape.

Just imagine. This was the way people talked around here. It sounded most peculiar, and Jon had difficulty fathoming what they were up to. It sounded as if they were having a fight over him.

Luckily, the exchange of words was interrupted by the fellow called Ricky, who appeared with a dented milk bucket filled with warm water and a bundle that turned out to be a huge worn-out wool sweater and a piece of cloth that had at one time been a curtain.

The sight of these objects caused the group to break out in laughter.

"Are you going to dress 'er up? Put 'er paws through the armholes? That'll be real sweet!"

"And she can have curtains at her windows, too!"

Jon felt confused by his role as intern. The onlookers crowded around him. He saw their faces only as light blobs, but he could sense grimaces and feelings that were very alien to his world. It seemed to him that their joking was teetering on the edge of violence. It made him think of two dogs he had seen one time playing along Three Hill Lane. They had been romping and yapping, but the next

44

minute, before you could turn around, they were fighting fiercely, growling and barking and showing their teeth. It was impossible to tell the point at which the change had taken place.

But the girl, Pixie's mistress, was absolutely undaunted.

"Out of my way, you guys. Don't crowd around like this. We can't take care of the little guys if you carry on like this!"

She jabbed her sharp shoulder blade into the side of the person standing next to her and, half sneering, half cursing, he recoiled.

"You, Ricky. You can help us," the girl added, nodding approvingly at the boy who had just successfully completed the mission of bringing the warm water.

The boy, thus favored and specially named, took the lid off the milk can. And as he did this, slowly, tenderly, with his head bent forward, as if the whole thing were a churchly rite, Jon became aware that something about his figure and his movements was familiar—something he had vaguely noticed earlier but that hadn't fallen into place in his mind.

Ricky. . . . Of course, this was a nickname for Rickard!

Of course. Why hadn't he recognized him immediately? This was Rickard—Rickard who sat in the farthest corner of the classroom and always paused a few moments before answering a question, but then, without exception, answered correctly. Rickard, who always won all the games and the gymnastic competitions, although you'd never believe it to look at his lanky, almost disjointed body.

Jon felt a sense of unhappiness coupled with embarrassment, partly because he hadn't recognized Rickard at

45

once and partly because he felt as if he had come upon a shabby secret by finding this boy, admired and even envied by everyone at school, in this notorious house.

Yes, it was true that Rickard—at the Martell School no one called him Ricky—was the object of much admiration and not a little envy. Even though he walked with his head bent forward and his chin almost on his chest, he was still a head taller than his classmates. Even though he read so slowly that it gave Jon the creeps to listen to him, he was praised for his sureness, his pronunciation, and his mode of expression. And though he was neither very well built nor muscular to any degree, he could use his spindly arms and legs as no one else in the class could.

"Hi, there!" Jon said as unobtrusively as possible, not wishing to arouse the curiosity of the other bystanders.

As usual, there was a pause before Rickard spoke. He was pulling himself together.

"Hi," he replied in an equally low voice. Then he added after a pause—and his few words were followed by a heavy sigh, which Jon also recognized from the classroom—"I live here."

Jon searched in vain for something more to say. It was just the way it was at school. So many times he had wanted to say something sharp, something funny or quick-witted —something that might have broken the ice and led to kidding and joking, and perhaps even friendship, with this interesting, somewhat forbidding Rickard. As usual, he had to give up the idea.

The girl, who disapproved of this little interlude, was tearing the curtain into smaller pieces.

"Give me a hand!" she yelled angrily. "Otherwise, the

water's jus' gonna stand there and get cold. Listen, you guys . . . !"

With some effort she and Jon managed to tear up the curtain. If you folded the pieces, they would do very well. Dipping them in the water, they washed and dried and rubbed the newborn puppies. Even the puppy with the white spot on its tail was breathing evenly and visibly now.

Meanwhile, Rickard slowly and purposefully spread out the woolen sweater on top of the blanket, and when the puppies were handed to him, he wound them in the sweater, rolling them back and forth as if he were kneading bread dough.

He did all this with the utmost gentleness, and Jon was fascinated with Rickard's hands. He had never paid any attention to them before. The fingers were bony and long, but they moved surprisingly masterfully and softly.

"We really should have some milk for them," Rickard said thoughtfully.

"Pixie has milk to give them herself!"

Nervously, the girl tugged at her long sweater so that it almost reached to her knees.

"It's plain as day that their mama can feed them. But they have to stay here with her and suck and suck until the milk comes. That's the way they do it; I know good and well. But I can't take them all upstairs together. Maw would have a fit. And Paw. He just came home!"

Suddenly, the mental picture of the drunken man who had crawled through the mud out there on the street was vivid in Jon's mind. Could it be possible that the man was somebody's father—this girl's father?

This was not necessarily so, but Jon began to realize it

might be difficult indeed to find a roof to put over the heads of the brand-new mother and her puppies.

Rickard's controlled, thoughtful voice came to the fore again.

"It was stupid to try to keep them alive. Pretty soon they'll have to have food—real food—milk, meat, and vegetables. Animals need all that nourishment, too. And who can afford to give them any food in this house?"

There was the heavy sigh again. Jon cast a sidelong glance at Rickard. The sigh sounded as if it had come from the depths of the soul of an elderly person.

Jon noticed that Rickard didn't speak as did Pixie's owner and the other young inhabitants of this depressing house. The Martell School had clearly influenced his method of expressing himself. Was this the reason, perhaps, that Rickard always spoke so slowly? Maybe his manner of speaking was not his own but something that had been cultivated and formed with great care.

An uneasy silence settled over the group.

"Milk and meat!" came a scornful voice from the back row. "You're outa your mind. At our house there hasn't been a drop of milk since last week, and that was sour!"

A mutter of general agreement followed the remark.

Suddenly, the girl began to cry. And how she cried! Clenching her small fists, all dirty and streaked after bathing the puppies, she pressed them to her face and alternately sobbed and wailed, "Stop your kidding, you lunkheads! We put some life in 'em and now they'll starve to death— that is, if somebody isn't kind enough to kill them, of course!"

Jon was taken aback. The whole situation was awful. He

had been dragged into it dismally unprepared; he had never known that problems of this sort existed. He saw before his eyes the big cans of milk from the Vidinge Dairy that were delivered to his house, the crocks and jars on the shelves in the cellar. He had often watched Mari skimming off the cream with a long-handled ladle, scooping off the heavy, thick whipping cream for berries and applesauce and other goodies . . .

Like a shot it hit him. Everyone in that dark, ugly courtyard was looking at him. There were different sorts of looks. He couldn't really see them, but he sensed them plainly; some of the looks expressed wonder, admiration, jealousy, some were piercing, demanding, scornful, dangerous.

Jon wiped his hands on his heavy winter coat. "The puppies," he thought. "It's a matter of their welfare. And Pixie, too. They are living things, all three of them. They're the ones we've been struggling for. I don't care how they all look, but it's a shame about the puppies . . . and the girl."

"I'll ask my father," he said. "Perhaps we can take them with us."

He was afraid that what he said sounded too sure, too superior, so he added hastily, "Perhaps we can't keep them ourselves, but the stonemason's place right beside ours has stables and storerooms of all kinds, and I'm sure there will be room there. And it's warm, too. We keep Figaro in their stable. Well, we can do that for the time being, anyway."

"Figaro. Is that your horse?"

"Yes."

At this point the voices sounded eager.

"I've seen you and your old man riding around lots and lots of times."

"I've seen both the gig and the sleigh! It's real elegant. Is it real silver there by the driver's seat and the other seat up front?"

"Silver?" Rickard said drily. "You're out of your mind. You wouldn't have silver on a sleigh! It's steel. Fine, highly-polished steel . . ."

"Well, maybe not on the doctor's sleigh. But there *are* silver trimmings on some sleighs! And the Vidinge patron has a coat of arms on his, I'm sure, and on his weapons and everything. A man like that has very elegant stuff."

Rickard snorted. He turned his back on the group, which seemed to have begun discussing their favorite subject.

"Take Pixie with you, and I'll carry the puppies out. They're very comfortable inside the sweater. We can carry them out to the gig, can't we?"

Jon caught Rickard's quizzical, businesslike look.

Inwardly, he knew that he had handled this whole matter a bit recklessly. He really had no idea what Father would say—and Mother, when they got home! But the part about the stables over at the stonemason's was true. And he had been careful to say "for the time being!"

Jon nodded curtly, and the procession began to move— the girl leading Pixie by a rope, Rickard with the bundled-up puppies, Jon, and the rest of the group.

Just as they passed the entrance at the corner of the court-yard, the door opened and Jon's father emerged, his little brown medical bag in hand. The metal fittings on the side of the bag gleamed in the gas light.

50

In a twinkling Jon could tell that his father looked a little strange. He had watched him return from so many house calls that he could usually puzzle out his frame of mind, because Father was not one to put on a false front. He could be exhilarated, jovial, thoughtful, absent-minded, red from overexertion, or deeply serious, but you could always tell which from his bearing.

This time he was pale, his skin in sharp contrast to his short, clipped beard. His forehead was glistening beneath his black fur hat.

Then Jon realized that Father was perspiring—to such an extent that drops were falling down over his eyebrows. His eyes seemed to have sunk into their sockets.

Jon halted. The gang of children and young people halted. Pixie strained at her rope.

It seemed as if Father didn't recognize Jon immediately, as if he had been away on a long trip and had to return to his surroundings gradually.

"Jon! What are you doing in here?"

Never once had Jon experienced the slightest fear of his father. Ten years of complete trust could not be wiped out at the drop of a hat.

"Well, this dog just had puppies in the courtyard there," Jon said as the group around him maintained a respectful silence. "Pixie is her name."

But it wasn't as easy as Jon had imagined it would be to blurt out an explanation. His father's tall, bent figure, his facial expression, so easily understood by Jon, betraying obvious exhaustion, aroused in Jon a feeling of uncertainty. Yet he had no choice. Not with Rickard and all the others standing there listening—curious but also suspicious.

"They can't keep the dog here," Jon said softly. "They don't have any food for her and they're very crowded— they don't dare show her puppies at home. So I told them that we could probably take them for the time being, either at home or in the stables over at the stonemason's—now that we rescued them and kept them alive and everything!"

By this time they had reached the gig; Father had not stopped walking.

Jon glanced at him out of the corner of his eye. Surely he would understand that something had been accomplished in there in that filthy courtyard—both by Pixie and the people who had helped her. Father couldn't help being pleased by the puppies, could he?

Figaro snorted and shook his harness, displeased at having been left alone out there on the street.

Father said, in a voice that sounded neither happy nor unhappy but as if his mouth were inordinately dry, "Well, I guess it will be all right. Put them down on the floor in back. But wait. Let me put my bag in first."

His tone of voice commanded a certain respect; everyone stood off at a distance but not so far that they couldn't hear. Pixie seemed to have succumbed to a fit of doubt and anxiety over what was about to happen to her. The girl whispered uneasily as she shoved Pixie into the gig, "Up with ya, stupid dog! Up with ya. Your puppies are gonna be with ya, and everythin's gonna be all right!"

Father grabbed the reins. Turning his head slightly as the gig began to move, he said, in his usual friendly manner, "We'll look after her properly! Run along now, children. Go on up and warm yourselves by the kitchen stove!"

But not until they were halfway across the deserted market square did he really come to life. Taking out his enormous checkered handkerchief, he wiped his forehead and cheeks.

"So, Jon, you had your duties tonight, too. As for me, I got there just in the nick of time."

Jon recalled that the midwife had arrived.

"Did somebody . . . somebody get born up there, too?"

Father nodded. His white teeth glistened. Jon knew that he had regained his composure.

"Was it awful? Did everything go all right? Did the baby live?"

Father laughed suddenly. "Yes, everything went fine. But it was touch and go for a while. I don't believe I've ever experienced anything like this before. For a while I thought there was going to be a very sad ending to the story."

"But you should be happy now—now that everything is all right."

"Yes, now that I have time to think about it, I am glad. But I think we'd better go directly home. I've got to wash up. I'll go to Helge Ridge afterwards. It was a lucky thing that we went where we did first. And you'll have to stay home, my boy, and take care of the dogs. Get something to eat and then see to it that you get yourself bundled off to bed!"

FOUR

Pixie and the puppies found shelter in an empty stall in the stonemason's stable. Mari was so violently opposed to having the new boarders in her kitchen that both Mother and Jon had to give in. Actually, Mother was the one who seemed most disappointed. Mother was just like a little girl when it came to children and animals—that was what Father always said. She was completely charmed by Pixie and her children.

"My heavens, Jon. How clever of you to be able to help her! Oh, they're just irresistible, especially this tiny one with its impertinent white tail!"

Mother held the puppy high above her head, just as she did Little Brother.

It was at that point that Mari, whose disapproval of the whole thing had been mounting steadily, came forth with the real clincher.

"What," she asked, "just *what* is the nurse going to say?"

Mother lowered her arms. Pixie must have realized that the fate of her children hung in the balance, because she began to bark wildly.

Sticking his hand inside his shirt, Jon began to scratch—first his back and then his arms.

Mari took a couple of backward steps and scored another telling point.

"Good gracious heavens! Can't you see how Jon is scratching himself? And I'm beginning to itch, too. Here . . . and here! The dog has fleas. Everyone does in those dreadful shacks on Quarry Road—both animals and people!"

"Fleas!" Mother repeated. "Yes, I guess Mari is probably right. The best thing is to put them in the stable. Take them outside, Jon, quick, quick!"

And Pixie *did* have fleas—a whole colony of them, some of which had already found a haven on Jon.

There was *some* bathing going on at the doctor's house that evening. First Pixie and the puppies were bathed out in the stable. Then Jon and Mari each had a bath in the huge tub out in the washhouse, and finally the doctor and his wife bathed in the tub in their own bathroom, which had to be filled with hot water carried from the kitchen but which was much admired and considered the height of modern fashion.

The nurse was the only one who escaped. But as she expressed it, she had "withdrawn" to her own room before the arrival of the dog family and was blissfully unaware of what she had missed.

All of them—Father and Mother, Mari and Jon—indulged in a completely deliberate conspiracy against the nurse.

"Don't breathe a word to her about the fleas!" Mother pleaded. "And if she should happen to begin to itch, she *could* have caught them from one of the patients, right?"

"Yes, of course, madam. This has happened before—it even happens in the hospital—and she really couldn't complain about that!" Mari assured her.

Mari and Jon almost laughed themselves sick afterwards in the washhouse. They could just picture the nurse attacking the fleas with all her might.

By this time Pixie and the puppies were fast asleep on their straw and blankets out in the stable. Pixie had been given some warm milk and a pork heart, which Mari had happily offered to cook for her; both of the puppies had nursed so eagerly that their small stomachs were swollen almost to the bursting point. Soren had proven to be very helpful, and Figaro neighed with glee upon discovering that he was going to have company in the adjacent stall.

Warm and happy after his bath, Jon slept a dreamless sleep in his white metal bed.

But the next night, he had dreams that were both strange and inexplicable. He felt that he really should have dreamt about Pixie and the puppies, maybe even about that dreadful, unsteady drunken man, about the officious little girl, or possibly had a nightmare concerning dark alleys or runaway horses, which he usually had following an adventuresome journey with Figaro. But instead he dreamt about Rickard, the strange, overgrown boy from the slum environment.

In his dream, Rickard was standing high above him on a hill, calling to Jon to climb up after him and take in the wonderful view from the top. Rickard could see way off in the distance, he shouted—all the way to Finland, to Italy, to Australia with its kangaroos, and to the Middle East with its deserts, dromedaries and their foals. . . .

57

But no matter how hard Jon tried, he just couldn't catch up with Rickard. With his arms and legs he struggled but got nowhere. And Rickard cried out, "Hurry up, boy, hurry!" at which point Jon awakened, trembling with frustration, with a lump in his throat.

It was a peculiar dream that lingered long at the bottom of Jon's mind in the form of a hazy, formless concept—something that nagged at him and caused him uneasiness long after he had awakened. That day as he sat at his school desk, his mind was far away.

Rickard Svensson's desk was over by the far wall of the classroom. This was where the tall pupils sat—six of them altogether. Five of them were one or two years older than Jon, were sluggish and slow, and had a "hard time of it," as the expression went, so were repeating a grade or had begun school late.

Rickard was tall, but he was no older than he should have been for his grade. As a matter of fact, he was some months younger than most of his classmates.

Time and time again during the class period, Jon turned around and looked at Rickard over there in his corner. The more he observed him, the more curious he became about the boy from Quarry Road. What attracted him to Rickard he was unable to say, nor did he attempt to figure it out.

Actually, Rickard was an amazing boy. He was amazing in his answers, in his agility at competitions and games, in a certain unevenness of disposition that aroused antipathy and respect simultaneously.

Several of the boys in the class tried to imitate Rickard, to look grown-up and self-assured when a question came their way and to make the answer sound nonchalant and self-evident. But the latter was a little troublesome, especially when they weren't genuinely sure of the answer.

It was easier to copy Rickard's clothing and other possessions. The minute Rickard began carrying his schoolbooks in a narrow feed sack that he had cut in half, the others began to regard their schoolbags with their long leather shoulder straps as old-fashioned and childish. Feed sacks were in great demand at the open market and in the shops.

About that time a small, dilapidated shop, which actually dealt mostly in heavy work clothes, began to stock a kind of checkered wool jacket that was displayed in the filthy, overcrowded window facing the street.

The children in the Martell School would scarcely ever have noticed these wool jackets if Rickard hadn't one day appeared in one. The checkered material was dark in color —you could make out rust, brown, and black—and the jacket was baggy and hung down around the hips.

A whole flock of eager boys and a few girls, together with their rather doubtful mothers, began to visit the little shop on Fishing Plaza. The jacket was so low priced that few mothers put up any serious objections, in spite of the sleazy, rough quality of the material. One checkered jacket after the other appeared in the classrooms and corridors of the Martell School. Those who wore them were proud; they considered themselves among the elite.

Jon dragged Mother down to Fishing Plaza. This was no great strain because Mother liked shopping for clothes and was interested in seeing the latest things. New models were few and far between in Soltuna.

But when she saw the location of the shop and stood outside looking in the dirty window at the messy piles of striped shirts, boots, and a number of padded waistcoats with the lining showing through, she was horrified.

"But, Jon, a lot of this clothing is definitely second-hand. Can't you tell that?"

"Some of it, sure. But not the jackets I have in mind, Mother. Look. Here they are!"

The garment he so desperately wanted had actually been removed from the window and was now hanging from a hook and flapping in the breeze, outside the shop, but Mother merely tugged at her skirts, revealing the pointed toes of her narrow, elegant leather shoes.

"Those things? Ugh! My dear child, can't you see that the material is no good at all? Picture yourself when it gets cold—really cold in the winter. The wind would blow straight through it. No quality to it at all."

"But, Mother, it's so big, that jacket, that I could wear two or three heavy sweaters under it. The other fellows in the class all do!"

"Absolutely out of the question!" Mother said, and these were words that seldom passed her lips. She was always trying to please Jon, to see things and events through his eyes, to be concerned, puzzled, and enthusiastic with him, and these things were fairly easy for her because she was young—not even thirty yet.

"Jon, you know perfectly well you have a fine coat, made of excellent material, with a new fur collar on it and everything! And, Jon, please don't say 'fellows.' That is a slang word, and it sounds perfectly dreadful. Father doesn't like it, as you well know!"

They left Fishing Plaza in a depressed frame of mind, an unusual thing for both of them. To make everything all right again, Mother took Jon to Rolander's Coffee and Pastry Shop and treated him to pastries and a soda.

The pastries they chose were pieces of sponge cake with vanilla icing between the layers. Both Mother and Jon were especially fond of this particular kind and were in complete agreement that the other pastries were quite unappetizing, displayed, as they were, in the shape of a fan on a tall-based white platter.

Back of the high counter, which was painted white, were mirrors that reached from floor to ceiling and that were framed in white and gold. The soda foamed in Jon's glass. He and Mother each sat in a plush-covered easy chair, and the little round table between them was white marble. The waitresses were dressed in white blouses and light blue skirts, which hung to the floor, with starched rosette-trimmed aprons and little caps on their heads. Rolander's Coffee and Pastry Shop was very attractive—almost as elegant as the Grand Hotel next door.

The episode at Fishing Plaza vanished from their minds but was replaced by a certain preoccupation on Jon's part. The checkered jacket had revealed something to Jon. He was not free; he didn't have the right to choose what he wanted. Father and Mother were right in what they had to say about quality, utility, and appropriateness. But there were times when you wanted to choose your clothing for other reasons.

The bubbles from the soda began to tickle Jon's nose. He couldn't bring himself to believe that Rickard had had either his father or his mother with him when he bought his jacket.

"In the spring," Mother said, "we'll get you a new light coat, Jon. We'll get the same material Father has in his. It's so stylish, and it will wear forever!"

The next day it happened that Jon was right behind Rickard as the whole class rushed headlong down the steep steps leading to the street at the end of the class period. The steps were very steep indeed, because the school building was built on a hill; on the side facing the street, there was one story more than there was on the other side.

Rickard's checkered jacket flapped behind him. As usual, he was among the first down the steps. The children always raced to see who would be first out of the huge glass doors and down onto the street.

Jon hadn't exchanged a single word with Rickard since they had met on Quarry Road. He felt that Rickard might at least have asked how Pixie and her puppies were. In any case, they had shared an experience that nobody else in the class even knew about.

Suddenly, Jon was struck with an impulsive, wild wish. He scarcely understood what was happening, but it hit him like an electric shock.

"Why can't Rickard and I be friends? He's exciting; he's different. I want to get to know him the way some of the other boys do—they yell and laugh and play ball together. I'm sure it's just because I haven't tried that I'm not included . . ."

Jon's hand flew out and grabbed the fast-moving jacket. He meant this as a friendly gesture, and simultaneously he called, "Hey, are you going over to the ball field?"

The words were also meant to sound relaxed and friendly. But for some reason, they tumbled from his mouth in the form of a breathless shout with a hint of command in it.

Horrified, Jon listened to his own voice. It had been all wrong—like the blare of a trumpet. At that very moment, Jon could hear the rip of a seam in Rickard's jacket.

Both boys stood stock still, Rickard one step below Jon. And this time there was no pause preceding his answer. It came out like a shot.

"Let go of me! You'll tear my jacket to pieces! There

are people who can't afford to buy new clothes any time they feel like it—good quality stuff with a fur collar on it!"

With utmost haste Jon had released his grip. Now he simply stood and stared. He wanted to say something about how neat he thought Rickard's jacket was—how much he preferred Rickard's jacket to his own coat. . . . But he had no chance to do anything more than stare and look puzzled in the few seconds when it might have been possible. The next minute Rickard's strong, gangly legs were carrying him rapidly down to the gate, through which he vanished.

A number of his classmates had witnessed the incident as they ran past. Now they glanced back at Jon from the gate. Their looks were filled with amazement, wonder, and curiosity, for the most part. Jon blushed furiously. He straightened his school cap, which had come to rest at an angle, and rushed past them. He began to whistle a march tune, looking neither to the right nor to the left.

He didn't go to the ball field. He never wanted to go there again. He walked directly home, and even when he crossed his own yard, he still felt a burning sensation in the region of his cheekbones.

It occurred to him that Rickard was jealous of him because his family could afford to buy things that Rickard's couldn't even dream of. The whole thing was absurd. Here they were, being jealous of one another, he and Rickard. "What a shame that you can't exchange the objects that make you jealous," Jon thought, "just as you can exchange book marks!" That way, both of them would have been happy.

Why couldn't they discuss things? Father was always saying that people should talk things over when they were of different opinions. But Jon recalled Rickard's flashing eyes, the scornful expression around his mouth. Evidently there were things that couldn't be discussed.

FIVE

Meanwhile, there was something else for Jon to think about when he reached the path leading to his home.

The gig was already standing outside the porch steps, and Figaro was saddled and ready to go. Soren was putting up the carriage top. It was a little unmanageable, with its edges flapping in the strong northwesterly wind. This sort of wind always picked up speed as it crossed the valleys to the north, finally sweeping across the doctor's yard, the stonemason's place, and Three Hill Lane.

It was already well into November; the piles of leaves had been burned, and the grass was frostbitten. It crackled and squeaked beneath your feet as you walked across it.

"Are office hours over already?" Jon asked Soren.

"An emergency call came, and the doctor wants to get going as quickly as possible. She, the nurse, had to tell the patients to come again tomorrow for their examinations and to have their dressings changed."

Over the years, Soren had learned a good bit about sickness and medical care and had begun to use the proper terminology. It seemed to him that this gave him added prestige among the other stable boys and apprentices.

"The doctor has to go out toward Vidinge to visit a crofter at Sea Gate whose leg got cut off in the woods."

"He didn't get it cut clear off, did he?"

"No, not really. I understand that there's a possibility of saving it. By the way, your mother has company."

Jon remembered that his mother was having some ladies in for coffee today. Suddenly, he was in a desperate hurry. If he didn't rush, he would be running the risk of Father's leaving without him and of being called in to say hello to the ladies. Through the half-open door leading to the dining room, he could see the apothecary's wife in a bright red dress with a feather boa over her shoulders and a plumed hat on her head.

His mother would make him comb his hair and plaster it down, and he would have to put on a clean collar!

Jon seized the steaming cup of hot chocolate that had been put out for him in the serving pantry. Mari's cookies and sweet rolls were richer than usual; he could tell by the taste. Jon had no intention of ignoring them. On the plate beside his cup were samples of all the kinds being passed around to the guests. There were cakes, pastries, marzipans, and walnut cookies.

But as far as Jon was concerned, they might as well have been salt pork and peas. He stuffed the food into himself as if he were stoking a furnace. If he did not drink the hot chocolate and eat something, he would not be allowed to go along. And since this was an emergency house call, Father wouldn't wait any longer than necessary.

Jon swallowed the last drop of chocolate, keeping an anxious ear turned toward the reception room. Now he could hear Father's voice. He was talking with the nurse about putting some disinfectant on the floor. Perhaps there had been some patient there today with measles, whooping cough, or scarlet fever.

Mari, who knew what was in the cards for Jon, came hurrying along and handed him a round box containing his shiny brown leather cap with the fur brim, which almost came down over his ears.

This was a thoughtful gesture on Mari's part, because she had a lot of extra work to do in connection with the coffee party. At least ten or twelve ladies were there, and the smell of freshly brewed coffee filled the kitchen.

His winter hat had been stored in mothballs, and both Jon and Mari got tears in their eyes from the strong odor as she shook it out.

" 'By now, Mari! And thanks ever so much!" Jon yelled from the hallway.

At that same second, Father appeared, moving with straight, sweeping gestures; his riding coat was as yet unbuttoned, and he carried his brown bag in one hand. He smelled of ether. From the reception room came the smell of strong disinfectant.

Jon tagged along at his father's heels, enjoying the smells. He could hear the shrill voices of the ladies and the rattle of the coffee cups clear through the walls.

Thank heavens, he had been rescued from the world of ladies and children; he was greatly relieved to have escaped. He belonged in the world of men, the world of strength, where voices were deliberate and deep.

It was doubly important for him to keep his place in the masculine world today. Rickard's words had seemed to him

68

a secret accusation that he was somewhat of a sissy. Fine quality material, fur collar. How awful! The dreadful words had hung in the air.

"Is the feed bag full?" Father asked. "Did you loosen Figaro's belly bindings? Did you put an extra candle in the equipment box? Oh, dear. I think I left my new stethoscope on the desk as I rushed out. Run in and get it!"

Jon flew like a bird. When he returned, all was in readiness, and Father sat with the reins in hand. Soren held the carriage apron open, and Jon hopped right in. Soren fastened it again once he was in, and Father stuffed the stethoscope down inside his riding coat.

It was dusk. Soren yelled "giddap" at Figaro, whose nostrils flared at the ether smell. It was like a battle sign to him. They were ready to take off!

The wind lashed at the honeysuckle vines; a pink bud, which would almost certainly never bloom, was visible among the dark leaves of the rose bushes.

"The last rose of summer," said Father. "Listen, Jon. When we get back home, you'll have to snip it off and take it in to Mother."

Figaro took off at a trot. They turned the corner by the Grand Hotel and drove along the carriage path through the city park. The wheels and hoofs thundered as they rolled across the wooden bridge spanning the Tun River.

Outside the hotel a carriage for hire had stood, and from the tavern door they could hear shouting and laughter, and a few figures had been visible; but apart from this, they saw no carriages, no sign of life.

A few unkempt red cottages, in bad shape but still inhabited, constituted the border line between the town and the country. They drove past a farmyard that looked well kept, after which they rode through the big woods.

The last light they passed was a flickering lantern in a barnyard. After that, all was total darkness on both sides of the road.

"How did the message arrive, Father?" Jon asked. He snuggled into one corner so as to sit more comfortably and safely, for the road was bad and the gig shook dreadfully in spite of its rubber tires.

"It came by telephone from Vidinge," Father said. "The old patron himself called. They are clearing the woods down by Vidar, and he has a couple of sawyers working for him there."

"Could you hear all right?" Jon wondered aloud.

The telephone was as yet a rather new invention, restricted to the richest of the merchants, city officials, and the doctor. The wires hadn't even been installed out in the country, but there was one at Vidinge, the district's only large, landed estate.

"Yes, for that matter, I heard pretty well. Lucky thing that the accident happened at Vidinge so that someone could get to a telephone. It will be a good thing when the system gets enlarged. It will save a good many lives, believe me!"

"We're inside the Vidinge Estates by now, aren't we?"

"I imagine so. This along here is called Vidinge Woods. There's a lot of wealth in these woods. The patron is very fortunate. And when the trunk line from the main railroad at Lina Sea is finished next year, he's going to be able to

70

make deliveries from his sawmills in a very different fashion, I would bet."

"He must be terribly rich, the patron," Jon said with a certain reverence in his voice. He could see row upon row of tree trunks on both sides of the road. It was almost like riding through a colossal colonnaded hall. The tops of the pines formed a cathedral-like arch across the road, Jon knew, having often been on that road in the daytime in an open carriage. Although Father, in conversation, called the owner of the Vidinge Estates "the patron," he was on a first-name basis with the man. There must have been thirty years' difference in their ages, but Father was a combination of both doctor and friend to the patron, as he was with many other people less well endowed.

Now and then Mother was also invited to the Vidinge Estates, and since this usually happened in the winter, the Vidinge sleigh with its coat of arms—the one that caused such a stir on Quarry Road—would come to call for her.

"The sawmill could develop into a huge enterprise if it's well managed—if the woods are cleared at just the right speed and reforestation is properly planned for. The patron told me today that he was going to have to hire additional people—young people whom he could train so that they would be ready the minute transportation can be had on a big scale."

"Father," said Jon, "do you think it's possible that he might need a new dog, too?"

Father laughed heartily.

"You have in mind Pixie's puppies, of course. They seem very nice, but it would be anybody's guess as to what breed

their father was. I can at least bring up the subject next time I see him."

"One of them, the female, is already spoken for," Jon said proudly. "Soren wants to keep her. And if the other one could find a home at Vidinge, everything would be great."

"What about Pixie herself?"

"The girl is going to take her back just as soon as the puppies can take care of themselves. She came up last night to see Pixie."

"You know," Father said, deep in thought, "it's funny how people operate, keeping dogs and cats although you can't imagine where they ever get hold of enough money to buy bread and milk."

They stayed on the so-called big country road for about three miles. After the woods came meadows, fences, and then more stretches of woods. They passed various small tenant farms, all owned by the Vidinge Estates, and gradually they arrived at the foot of the mighty Korp Mountain.

Jon was well acquainted with the road, and both he and Father, and Figaro for that matter, knew exactly where they were, although it was pitch dark by now. Above the fences a weak light from the western skies had lingered, and you could make out the contours of houses, haystacks, and windmills. But as they drove in under the projecting rocks, all semblance of daylight disappeared.

Figaro began to speed up. There were elks along here—maybe he had already picked up the scent, or maybe he was recalling an encounter with the huge gray animals along this stretch of the way. Figaro wasn't happy in this territory.

73

To the left of the road, on this stretch between the mountain and the long lake called Vidar, was a village consisting of half a dozen low gray cottages and a yellow mission house. All that could be seen of the village now were two or three dimly lighted windows, and these disappeared as soon as the gig hit the brush forest.

At this point they were beginning the ascent. Along here brooks originating on Korp Mountain came rushing and roaring down the hills and, in the spring, rocks, carrying with them sand and gravel and leaving deep ruts along the way. The gig shook as it went over the ruts and, now and then, over rocks, the surface of which had been worn round and smooth by the ice of thousands of springs.

They were still on the big country road leading to Vidinge, but on the other side of the mountain, it ran into a lovely chestnut-lined avenue, which led to the living quarters.

"Peculiar," Father remarked, "that they don't take better care of this road. This is the way all the guests of the estates have to come—all the merchants, and some of them bigwigs at that. But there is a shortage of workers, and the ones they can get are needed to work in the forests."

"But couldn't the patron hire people from the city?" Jon inquired. "There are lots of people who don't have jobs. Just think of all the people who live in the building on Quarry Road. They need to earn money, don't they?"

"Well, you'd think so," Father said. "But—in the building Pixie came from—there are a great many good-for-nothings who drink a lot and who have no desire for steady work, especially a heavy job like road work. And they wouldn't be much good at it, for that matter. They don't keep themselves in condition; they have no muscles."

"But what do they live on?" Jon wanted to get to the bottom of this, aware that it might help to solve the mystery surrounding Rickard. "They've got to have some way of bringing home money, don't they?"

Father didn't answer right away. They sat warm and sheltered, he and Jon, in their own little comfortable world. The flame of the gig's lantern fluttered violently when the gig shook, and the glow illuminated the red velvet of the carriage apron, the blue cushions, the leather fittings, and the polished handles.

But just beyond the carriage was the darkness—heavy and impenetrable—encompassing all sorts of unforeseen possibilities and dangers.

Father was hesitant. He was so accustomed to speaking straight from the heart, as was Jon, that he was inclined to forget the boy was still only ten years old.

Perhaps he shouldn't frighten the boy, shouldn't bring him face to face with life's darkest side. Jon knew about sickness and need—more so than most of his contemporaries from well-to-do homes. But was it necessary, was it wise to tell him about crime, which was on the increase, about real dangers that could threaten them on the roads and in the streets?

Father's desire to be completely honest with his son won out. He didn't want to treat him as a child. Perhaps he unconsciously saw in him a certain support—someone with whom he could speak frankly.

"You see, Jon," he said, slackening his grip on the reins

and letting them fall to his lap. "It's very difficult for the police to catch them and begin to clear out the worst places inside the city limits. It just so happens that a lot of them support themselves by pilfering and theft, by means of robbery and assault. Soltuna has grown a good bit since the stone industry became a big thing, and a mass of rather doubtful characters followed in the backwash of the honest-to-goodness workers, of whom there are many. For the time being, there is a surplus of laborers, and a number of weak-willed characters among the unemployed have fallen into bad company. Then they form into bands.

"There have been several houses broken into since the autumn darkness began in earnest. Last week a bank clerk was robbed on the way from the hotel to the county bank. He had a couple of thousand *kronor* with him, and he was half dead when they found him. They called me from the hotel, and I drove the boy to the hospital myself."

"Oh, I remember," Jon said eagerly. "They called you in the middle of dinner, and you just took off without saying a word."

"The boy is going to pull through," Father went on, "but they'll never see hide nor hair of the money again. And they haven't been able to find a trace of the thieves. They had dumped the boy off in the bushes at the far corner of the city park, and one of the lamplighters heard him moaning.

"The jewelry and watch shop was the site of a robbery just before that. It appears to have happened in the middle of the night, and it was discovered when daylight came."

"Did they get anything?"

"Well, there wasn't much money. They took it all, of course. And in addition, every gold watch."

"But what were they going to do with all the watches? If they sold them around here, they would be discovered immediately and put in jail, wouldn't they?"

"It's too bad in a way that the main railroad is so near. Either they ride up to Stockholm or over to Denmark and sell them there, or else they deliver them to a middleman who will pay them perhaps half of what they are worth."

For a while Father was silent.

"I've got to be on the alert," he said. "We have to turn up a little path through the forest, off to the left down toward Vidar Lake, and I don't want to drive past it. There—if I'm not mistaken, there it is."

As had happened so many times, Jon was amazed at his father's sense of direction. The gig squeaked and shook. The path was nothing more than a couple of deep ruts; it was a small clearing in the forest. The pine branches brushed against the sides of the gig, and they could hear the mud splashing up against the bottom of the carriage. Father tightened his grip on the reins. You couldn't make out the holes in the road, and a broken axle would hardly be a joke this far away from any signs of life.

"Well, we're a long way from civilization," Father said. "On the main stretch of Vidinge Road, there are people riding along occasionally, even though we didn't meet any this evening. The traffic has increased with the expansion of the sawmills, and the robbers have discovered this fact, too.

"I spoke a few moments ago about robbery and assault—

the robbers concentrate on the main roads now that it gets dark so early. Several weeks ago the manager from Vidinge Estates was the victim of a holdup down by Korp Mountain."

"The place we just passed?" Jon asked breathlessly.

"The very place. But they got nothing that time. The manager had sent the weekly deposit to the bank with the patron himself earlier that day, because they had seen some strangers hanging around the area and had gotten suspicious. . . . You're not going to be afraid to ride in the dark hereafter, are you, Jon?"

"Not at all," Jon said boldly, and he meant it. He couldn't really imagine any danger lurking, any sort of accident happening as long as Father was by his side.

The woods thinned out. In the light of the lantern, they could see piles of timber that glistened a sort of rosy red. The tree stumps shone white.

The road sloped downward steeply. Father held Figaro back. Jon's eyes, searching the darkness, could make out the blackish water of the lake, and the contours of two of the crofter cottages were visible against the water, one in back of the other. They looked as if they were just one room and a kitchen. In the window of one of them, which faced the path, was a light. The ground around the gig was covered with pieces of bark and wood chips.

A door creaked in the cottage with the lighted window, and a figure with a lantern in hand could be seen on the bridge, the boards of which shook. Someone was swinging the lantern as a signal of welcome and anxiety. The shadow was a huge one, and you could tell that it was made by

78

someone wearing a kerchief and shawl. This must be the
crofter's wife, who had come to show the way.

"There's no place around here to put Figaro," Father
said as he unfastened the carriage apron and took out his
bag. "I don't think it's worth while for you to come in. The
old woman can no doubt give me all the help I am going
to need. Please spread the blanket on Figaro, Jon, and give
him a little something to chew on."

Jon didn't need to be reminded of the latter. Among the greatest pleasures in Jon's life, and preferably in the quiet of the forest near the lake, was petting Figaro's soft nose and feeling the teasing muzzle against the inside pocket of his coat—the place where Jon kept coarse, hard bread and sugar lumps.

Another light appeared at the cottage door. Father's deep voice, never unnecessarily brisk, always considerate and able to inspire complete trust, was blended with the woman's, piercing and shrill because she was excited and worried. She managed to let out a veritable stream of words before the door closed, at which point the silence of nature was in complete control.

SIX

Figaro and Jon had to wait a long time in the little clearing in the forest down by Vidar Lake, but they were far from bored. They delighted in each other's company, and the chill of the evening wasn't bitter and penetrating, only pleasantly invigorating. A faint breeze—so faint that it didn't even rustle through the treetops—arose from the shiny black water. A cat, unable to command the attention it was used to, miaowed now and then over by the corner of the cottage. Jon didn't actually see the animal, although he tried to get it to come, but he sensed that soft paws were padding across the planks of the bridge.

Jon sucked on some licorice bits and cough drops, which he had fortunately bought in a nice, pleasant-smelling candy shop on Three Hill Lane that morning. As for Figaro, he munched first on some bread, and then on three sugar lumps. Having swallowed the latter, he began to lick his chops and wave his tongue. As the waiting time drew to an end, the heavy clouds dispersed, revealing a section of bright sky, alive with stars—a small preview of the endless wonders of the cosmic world—which shone down upon the water.

At last Father emerged. By the tone of the voices, Jon could tell the outcome. Father had accomplished his mission well: he sounded pleased—in fact, quite jovial. The old woman's shawl fluttered in the breeze, and you couldn't help but notice her grateful bows and curtsies. This meant that Father would be talkative and that the journey home would be a delight.

Jon removed the heavy blanket from Figaro's back, folded it, and stuffed it in under the seat. Figaro snorted. He was not particularly happy. He had hoped to find hay and oats at the bottom of his feed bag. But since they would be back home within the hour, he would just have to make do until then.

And so they started home again. Father turned up his fur collar, and Jon lowered the brim of his cap. The wind, such as it was, was against them, which, combined with the speed at which they were traveling, made the cold seem bitter, especially as it hit their cheeks.

The minute they were out of earshot, Father began to laugh. He threw his head back and roared so hard that he shook. His short black beard seemed to be standing straight up in the air.

"What about his leg?" Jon asked. "Had he really sawed off his leg as Soren told me?"

Father drew a deep breath.

"Heavenly days, no!" he said, but his laugh concluded with a sigh. "People get themselves into the strangest predicaments! Well, I'm going to tell you what happened to the man in the cottage, but it will have to be strictly between us, Jon. I feel sorry for these fellows. They aren't very well paid, these workers, and you can understand that

82

they try to make a little extra income whenever the opportunity presents itself. Of course, it's rather bad when they don't keep their activities within the law."

"I won't say a word, Father. You know that!"

"His leg hadn't even been touched. He had gotten his posterior full of buckshot!"

"But . . ."

"They were cutting down trees and sawing them into logs, this man and his friend, the one who lives in the other cottage. They're not too well off financially, as I mentioned. When they go out into the woods, they take their shotguns with them, and if they're lucky, something in the way of wildlife appears on the scene, and they lose no time in grabbing their opportunities. In these woods there are a good many deer and wild fowl. The men never bother with an elk. Fortunately for them, they don't have rifles with recoilers."

"But, Father . . . this wildlife belongs to the patron, doesn't it?"

"Naturally. They have no right to shoot at all, no doubt about that. And they do get some sort of punishment for their errors—that's the way it goes in this world. Today one of them sighted a grouse and shot, but he hit his friend, who was bending over a pile of timber. It wasn't a direct hit, of course, and the shots were pretty diffused, but he got quite a bit of lead in him, anyway."

"Oh, that must have hurt something fierce!"

"It certainly did! It was a shame about the fellow, but he'll soon recover; I took all the buckshot out, cleaned the wounds, and put bandages on. It could have been infinitely worse had he cut his leg, for example."

"But are you going to tell on him, Father? Tell the patron?"

"No. No, I'm not going to. The fellow swore that he would never shoot anything on the sly again. And now we can only hope that the temptation won't be too great in the event a black cock or pheasant flies in front of their noses. And you'll have to admit that the temptation would be pretty strong if the larder were empty at home. Sometimes they sell their bounty, under the table, somewhere in the city. They get as much as three *kronor* for a pheasant hen, and I imagine that's as much as or more than they earn per day."

"Father!"

"Yes?"

"There are an awful lot of things that aren't right—terribly unjust—aren't there?"

"Yes, you're absolutely right. But the laws of the land must be obeyed. Otherwise, where would we end up? The only thing to do is to fight for better conditions, for more equitable salaries. These workers aren't criminals—not by a long shot."

"So you've decided not to tell the patron, then?" Jon was still a little concerned.

"No, certainly not. Wouldn't do it for anything. It would only make matters worse. Both of the fellows were pretty upset and also contrite."

Father yawned. He took out his huge gold watch and held it near the lantern on the side.

"Half-past six. That's pretty late. A little food will taste good when we get home, don't you think?"

"Have you had anything to eat since breakfast, Father?"

"No, there just wasn't time. From what I could tell from the telephone conversation, the fellow was about to bleed to death. It was just sheer luck that I had pincers and all that with me and didn't have to take any stitches."

At this point the carriage swung off to the left, and the wheels skidded as they emerged from the deep ruts of the forest path. Once again they were on the big Vidinge Road.

Figaro began to trot at a good pace. He wanted nothing more than to return to the stable, eat his hay and oats, and bask in the warmth of his stall. Father had to hold him back at the hilly area at the foot of Korp Mountain. He loosened the reins as they emerged from under the overhanging rocks.

The road narrowed. Autumn rains had washed away a good chunk of the right side.

"Look, Father," Jon said, pointing upward. "Look up there. You can see the Big Dipper."

Father leaned forward a little in order to see over the treetops to the north.

And at that moment, it happened. Figaro took a violent leap to one side and reared up on his hind legs. The carriage crashed against a huge pile of gravel and tipped to one side. Jon was thrown against the corner of the gig, hitting his shoulder.

"Elks," Jon thought. "If Figaro starts to run wild . . . !"

"Dirty devils!" Father said, and Jon knew that Father was clenching his teeth under his black beard. He pulled on the reins with all his might.

This was an unnecessary gesture. The danger threatening

85

them was not that Figaro might try to run away. He had come to a dead stop, his head turned in an unnatural way. A long dark shadow appeared alongside him.

Something was pressing on the step on Father's side to such an extent that the whole gig rocked on its springs.

New shadows . . . faces . . . masculine faces in the uneasy, fluttery glow of the lantern. One face came very close. At first Jon thought the lower half of his face was covered with a heavy beard, but then he realized that the man had a handkerchief tied across the tip of his nose. He had a hat pulled down over his forehead, too, and all that could be seen of his face were his closely set eyes.

"Get out!"

"What do you want?"

"You'll soon find out. Get out, I said."

Jon, over in his corner, suddenly understood what it was all about. This was a band of robbers. He and Father had been attacked.

Unbelievable! Attack—this was a storybook word, having to do with adventure, with magic. It wasn't a word that belonged in the realm of reality—not to Jon, anyway.

Suddenly, he sat up straight. Imagine anyone's daring to talk that way to Father!

Father unfastened the carriage apron. With one foot on the step of the gig, he calmly dropped to the ground. On the way out, he stepped to one side to avoid a puddle of water. He drew himself up to his full height. He was a full head taller than the masked man.

But the latter was holding a big club in his hand. A couple of other shorter figures, with stocking caps on their

heads, drew near from opposite directions. One of them was leaning against a gun.

Jon clenched his fists. This—all of it—was in deadly earnest. He was boiling mad. He didn't feel little and insignificant. On the contrary, he felt that he had grown—that he wanted to fight back. He remembered Father's wallet, generally fat and round and stuffed with money. This was where he kept the day's receipts. A number of his patients paid cash—not the civil servants, of course, nor the quarry and brewery workers, because the bills for these patients were sent to their employers, but almost everyone else.

One of the shorter men inquisitively poked his nose under the cover of the gig.

"Leave the boy alone!" Father's voice broke the silence.

Strange to say, instead of being afraid, Jon felt anger mounting.

Reality certainly was different from adventure stories. He thought the fellows looked dirty and stupid. They were like good-for-nothings from some tenement district, not like highway robbers. You might even beat them up . . . ! But then there was the club . . . !

"We're not after sniveling brats. Where's your wallet? This is a holdup, don't you understand?"

They were nervous, fearful, and obviously in a hurry. Father's calculated movements, free from any opposition but painfully slow, irritated them. They almost jumped up and down in their impatience.

The wallet was chock-full, as usual. Father shouldn't have brought it along with him on that dark journey! But no doubt he was in such a hurry, and his mind was on the injured patient. And maybe he, like Jon, couldn't believe that an attack really would take place.

Now he held the wallet in one hand, but none of the men made any attempt to grab it. They exchanged uneasy glances. Probably they were cowards; none of them was a leader.

The masked man finally put his club under his arm. He had realized that this particular traveler wanted no part of violence. Reaching out his hand, he hesitantly took the wallet. It looked almost comical—as if someone were reaching for a package across a counter in a store.

But as his hands felt the thickness of the leather wallet, he gained a measure of self-confidence and shouted, "What about your watch!"

The others muttered approvingly.

Jon craned his neck. His throat was as dry as a bone.

Father's watch! The heavy timepiece of solid gold in its shiny case, with its engraved initials and other adornments! It glistened in Father's hand, and the heavy gold chain, which he usually wore across his vest, dangled.

Just as the masked man grabbed it, this time with a quick, almost predatory jerk, the strange ceremony was interrupted.

The man who had halted Figaro, the one Jon had thought of as an accessory or a sort of helper, stepped into the circle of light. He was dressed in what everyone referred to as a brewery uniform and wore a hat. He probably wanted to take a look at their haul as had his comrades.

The others' hands fumbled as they felt the weight of the watch and the thickness of the wallet. As the newcomer made his appearance, however, their movements became visibly more uncertain. They took a couple of steps back-ward.

Jon realized that he had been mistaken all along. This man was no mere accessory. He was a model of hardness, of a certain kind of courage—he was their leader. He didn't resemble the others, either; he hadn't bothered to cover his face, nor did he have the same dissipated look they had. He moved in an entirely different fashion, quickly, purpose-fully; he seemed tall and flexible.

The masked man, without a moment's hesitation, handed him the wallet and the watch. But the other man didn't take them. He wasn't looking at them. He was looking at Father.

Sticking his hand in his pocket, he brought out a box of matches and lit one of them. Jon jumped a foot. He held the flame close to Father's face, which, for a split second, was clearly illuminated. He saw the black beard, a glimpse of white teeth, the calm eyes underneath a wide forehead.

Then the unbelievable happened.

The man in the brewery uniform said, "Give the stuff back to him. This will never do!"

At first Jon didn't understand. He sidled along the seat all the way to the other side in order to see better.

Neither did the man's companions understand. They stood there in doubt and bewilderment.

"What the . . ."

"Shut up. This won't do, I said. This is the fellow who saved my old lady's life. This is the doctor, you lunkheads. Give the stuff back, I said."

While the others merely stood there looking nonplused,

he reached over, took the watch and the wallet, and placed them in Father's hand. Father had raised his head slightly.

In deep silence they looked at one another. Then the man in the brewery uniform cleared his throat.

"Step inside again, Doctor, and go on your way. The whole thing was a big mistake. We didn't recognize your gig in the dark."

Father maintained his silence. Using the same calculated movements that he had throughout the entire episode, he returned the gold watch to its place in his vest pocket and his wallet to the inside pocket of his jacket.

These were movements that Jon had seen him make hundreds of times—even thousands of times. They were signs of confidence that brought the whole scene back down to earth.

He began to button his riding coat, but he didn't immediately climb back into the gig. He remained standing as if he were weighing something in his mind. The four men, who a few moments before had seemed so overpowering, now stood respectfully before him. One of the shorter men had removed his stocking cap and was twisting it between his hands. They looked as if they expected some polite words of farewell, as if the wallet and the watch had never come near their clumsy fists.

Father bowed his head, just the way Jon had seen him do when he left a house where someone had died. Clearing his throat, he said, "And how is Mrs. Svensson? Did she recover fully? And how is your little boy?"

They were simple words, but Jon was aware of what his father was trying to convey. Even the man in the brewery uniform must have caught their significance. His voice sounded disturbed and fuzzy when he answered.

"Thanks, she . . . she's very well. And the boy is . . . a fine baby."

Father nodded. He said nothing more. The gig rocked beneath his weight as he climbed up and gave Figaro his signal. The four men stepped to one side as the horse took off. Jon leaned out and peered back along the road, but after a brief moment the motionless silhouettes of the robbers were swallowed up by the darkness.

SEVEN

There could be no doubt that Figaro was conscious that something improper and dangerous had taken place. He trotted at such a pace that his mane flew. You could just picture the whites of his eyes glistening uneasily as shadowy stones, tree stumps, and thickets appeared and disappeared. By now he sensed danger in every overhanging rock, around every turn in the road.

"There, there, boy!" Father said. "Well, Jon, what do you have to say about all this? Were you terribly frightened?"

He let out a little laugh, not exactly an appropriate answer to the question. He swallowed. Even yet he felt a certain dryness in his throat, the same sort he had felt when the watch was imperiled. His shoulder ached where it had hit the corner of the gig.

"A little," he admitted. "Not at first. I began by being angry. But then . . . it would have seemed so terrible to part with Grandfather's watch without doing anything about it. And it suddenly occurred to me that you might have similar thoughts . . . !"

"That might have gone very badly," Father said, deep in thought. "I should have had sense enough to leave the money and the watch at home. It was stupid of me to have had them along, but hindsight is always easier than foresight. Somehow you feel that all the talk about robbery and attacks being on the increase is wildly exaggerated and, well, that in any case nothing as wild as that could ever happen to you. I must say, Jon, we've learned a lesson!"

"Father, are you going to tell the police about this when we get to the city?"

Eagerly, Jon leaned forward. This might lead to some excitement! He had never been in the precinct office near the Town Hall. He might get to see what it looked like from the inside, might have to be a witness, perhaps even help capture the thieves and put them in jail.

Father stroked his beard. For a couple of minutes, he sat in silence.

"Humph," he finally said. "That's a real problem. The police would request us to describe the men. They'll surely ask if I can identify any of them."

"Iden . . . iden . . . do you mean if you recognized any of them? Well, you did, Father. You did! You recognized that man Svensson!"

"Yes, yes, of course I recognized him. But when it comes right down to it, he's the one we have to thank that we're still sitting here, you and I, and that we still have the money and the watch!"

"Father, is it true what he said—that you saved the life of his . . . old lady?"

"That's hard to say. She might have made it without any help from me. But it was a difficult delivery, and she was in a bad way when I arrived. As a matter of fact, it happened on the same evening that Pixie had her puppies. I'm sure you haven't forgotten that evening."

"I'll say not."

"But the baby would never have made it; that I can say definitely. There was no heartbeat when the little fellow made his entrance into the world. He was completely blue in the face and wasn't breathing at all. Mrs. Lundgren and I got him to breathe . . . only at the last possible moment."

"Father, are there several families named Svensson in the building on Quarry Road?"

Amazed, Father glanced at Jon.

"What do you mean? Not to my knowledge. Why do you ask?"

"There's a boy in my class at school whose name is Svensson, and he lives there. I met him out there in the courtyard that night. Do you think—you really don't think he could be this man's . . . *his* son, do you?"

Jon and Father looked at one another. Jon's mouth was wide open, as was usually the case when he had something serious to think about.

"Don't stare with your mouth open, Jon!" Mother was always saying. But Father never brought up the subject.

Figaro was holding a nice even tempo now as he trotted along. His hoofs pattered rhythmically. The road ahead seemed like an endless ribbon beneath the carriage, and the road behind disappeared in the shadows of the unidentifiable land.

"I know the boy," Father said after a moment's pause. "He's not the son of the man who tried to rob us; he's his brother. There are a whole flock of brothers and sisters—

eight or ten of them—and they all live together crowded in one of the hovels up over the courtyard. This Svensson probably doesn't have an apartment of his own, although he's married, so for the time being he's still living with his parents, and when he and his wife were expecting their baby, I guess they had no place to go."

They had reached the farmyards just outside the city limits. A couple of dim lights gleamed up on the hillside. Suddenly, Figaro let out a wild neigh. He knew that he had friends in one of the stable buildings, and he was delighted that, with the aid of his senses of smell and hearing, he could discern where he was.

"Actually," Father said casually, "I was the one who

recommended the elder Svensson's youngest boy for a scholarship to the Martell School. He could read by the time he was just under five, and he could spell out all the street signs. He read me an article from an old newspaper that his father had wrapped around a milk bottle. It had to do with the art treasures in the Vidinge Estates, I recall, and I must say that I doubt if he understood much of what he was reading, but he pronounced the words correctly without stumbling in the least."

Father laughed and then went on, "It was really comical to listen to him! Several of the Svensson children have good heads on their shoulders, but most of them haven't had much education, so they get into some situations in which they don't contribute much to society. What is his name again, your classmate? I seem to have forgotten."

"Rickard."

"Oh, yes, of course. Rickard. Tell me, how does he get along in school?"

"He's one of the best in the class. And terribly good at sports and gym and things like that."

"That's nice to hear. Now set me straight, Jon. Next fall you'll have to take exams for the Latin School, won't you?"

"Isn't it typical of Father not to be sure of a thing like that?" Jon thought. Mother always said that Father had too many things on his mind.

"You know perfectly well that I have to," Jon said tolerantly. "But what does that have to do with Rickard?"

"Well, just that it could be a little tricky to get him into the Latin School. There aren't many scholarships available, and the competition is dreadfully keen—among all the children from several districts around Soltuna."

"What's going to happen if he doesn't get a scholarship?"

"Well, he'll just have to go to one of the other schools, but they're not as good. It would be a shame now that he has gotten such a fine start."

Once more Jon's mouth was agape. He thought of the pupils at one of the other schools near his own—the way some of them fought and yelled and howled as they walked along Three Hill Lane. The candy shop wouldn't even allow some of them inside the door. He thought of the school building, which was not very attractive, of the schoolyard, which was enclosed with a high iron fence and which didn't have even a small flower bed or a bush anywhere. The whole school seemed to be hard and gray—as uninviting as the dull stone it was built of.

Martell School had a long, beautifully kept bed of flowers from one side of the grounds to the other. Crocuses and Easter lilies bloomed there in the spring, and in the autumn the place came alive with the tall sunflowers that have brown centers and brilliant golden petals.

It would be terrible to have to leave there and go to the other school. He could picture Rickard behind the iron fence with his face half hidden by the bars, the ends of which were sharply pointed. He could see Rickard standing there, looking after Jon and his other classmates as they wandered down the hill instead of up, toward the open market and the Latin School, which was located just opposite the Town Hall and which looked every bit as majestic and awe-inspiring as the hall itself.

It must be awful to be poor! The word had so many meanings—more than other words. You almost wished the word didn't exist.

Father must have been pondering, too. He had been quiet for a long while. Then he said, "This school business is something we've got to think about and remember. Jon, you'll have to remind me. We'll have to do something about Rickard. . . . But now we'll soon be home, and it will be nice after our adventure, right?"

"But what about the police, Father? Are you going to report the attack to them?"

Father stroked his beard.

"I've been giving it a good deal of thought. I think we're just going to keep this to ourselves. Actually, one good turn deserves another. Svensson was no doubt criticized by his comrades because they weren't allowed to keep their haul. And they'll never strike at the foot of Korp Mountain again —he's too shrewd for that. If they strike again, it will be somewhere else. And Svensson will keep himself away from Soltuna for a while; you can be certain of that. For that matter, we weren't robbed; nothing was stolen from us. I think I'll just let the whole matter drop. . . . But, Jon, please don't mention a word of this to Mother this evening, because she'll be so upset and worried. Sometime I'll tell her the whole story . . . but not now—not while we have the whole dark winter ahead of us and a good many night journeys, too."

Jon noticed that Father had said "we." He rubbed his sore shoulder and made up his mind never to say a word about the episode.

"I won't say anything, Father, and I won't tell the story to Soren, either, because he would spread it to Mari, and then Mother would hear all about it."

The latter was a great sacrifice on Jon's part. Soren was

usually a fine, interested listener when Jon was willing to tell him what he had seen, heard, and experienced out in the streets and on the roads.

At this point they turned in at the doctor's gate. Jon caught a glimpse of Mother's shadow between the curtains in the dining-room window. She was almost surely supervising the setting of the table for the evening meal. If emergency calls didn't interrupt, this was usually the best, most peaceful meal of the day.

Father held Figaro back. He was ready to go directly to his stall, carriage and all. Father said, "Jon, you cut off the last rose of the summer and take it in to Mother. Oh, here's Soren. Good evening."

Jon held out his hand, and Father handed him his pocket knife, which had, in addition to several blades, a corkscrew. It was not the first time he had been sent down to the garden to get a particular flower—a tiger lily, a stalk of bleeding hearts, or, as was the case now, a rosebud for Mother.

In the small square of light that came from the hall window, he found the flower easily. It was fun, out there in the half darkness, to run his finger cautiously up and down the thorny stem. The pungent smell of half-frozen earth combined with old dead grass hit his nostrils.

Jon lingered as he went up the few steps leading inside, pressing the bud against his nose but finding it scentless. He closed his eyes. All through the muscles and limbs of his body coursed a delightful sense of sleepiness. It seemed to him that everything but his sense of smell had been dulled. On the porch, which was a small veranda with a couple of wicker chairs, a table, and benches fastened to the wall, he could smell the trees and the candle wax from a huge candlestick, the base of which was imbedded in the sheet-metal latticework.

In the hallway the familiar smell of disinfectant lingered, added to which was the odor of kerosene from the huge lamp with the yellow shade, standing on the table below the mirror.

Finally he reached the living room, and the smells were overpowering to him. After all, he had just come in from the clear, cool evening air. Jon opened his eyes.

Mother said, "Mari is a perfect angel! In spite of the fact that she's had such long working hours today, she insisted that Father should have a genuine *smörgåsbord* tonight, as usual!"

Jon's eyes scanned the oval dining table that stood directly under the ceiling lamp with its kerosene well, which was suspended from three heavy chains.

He noticed serving dishes that contained sausages, tiny meatballs that were still sizzling hot, a platter of mushroom omelet, smoked ham, and thin, thin slices of tender white veal with dark brown gravy. He saw herring and potatoes, pickles, red beets, liver *pâté*, and smoked eel.

Through the door to the serving pantry, Mari emerged with a couple of dishes containing piles of butter almost big enough to be Christmas trees. Mother put down the breadbasket with slices of both soft and hard bread.

"Oh, thanks so much, Mari! The doctor will be here in a minute—he's just washing his hands. Oh, Jon, hurry and take off your coat and wash your hands, too, so that Father's food won't get cold! You must be as hungry as bears!"

Jon obeyed as if in a trance. The hunger, which had almost disappeared during their roadside adventure, came back now with a vengeance. When he returned to the dining room, both Mother and Father stood beside Mother's chair. He stood back of her, put his arms around her, and kissed her. This was nothing unusual—maybe the kiss just lasted a little longer than was generally the case.

Jon handed the rosebud to Mother.

"Oh, Jon, is that the last rose? Thank you. Thanks a million. I'll just pin it here on my dress. But now we simply must sit down . . . Mari is so worried that the food will get cold. Say grace, please, Jon."

And Jon said grace.

As he pulled his chair out, vivid pictures flashed through his mind . . . Korp Mountain, the men with the big club, their dirty, trembling fists. Where were they by now? Did they have anything to eat, any place to go where they could wash up and then sit in a warm, well-lighted room?

"I think we'll soon have snow," Father said as he unfolded a huge snow-white napkin.

"Jon, dear," Mother said. "Don't sit there with your mouth wide open. Help yourself to some bread, and please pass the meatballs!"

EIGHT

Father proved to be a true prophet. The first snow of the season fell that same week and, remarkably enough, remained on the ground, not melting as it usually did in the pale November sun. The nights were cold; the ground froze. The tall sunflowers outside the Martell School withered away as if they had been attacked by invisible flames, and with the coming of the snowstorm, the stalks broke. The mornings were so dark that the children saw no more than dim shadows of one another on Three Hill Lane. It happened occasionally that you didn't recognize one of your classmates until entering the schoolyard, though you had walked nearby up the entire length of the last hill.

New snow fell, putting an additional cloak of white on Soltuna's streets. The Saturday before the first Sunday in Advent, various unemployed citizens were hired as snow removers, and the brewery horses were hitched up to the heavy triangular wooden snowplows in order that the streets and the marketplaces could be made passable.

That was the Saturday when they sang "Oh, Blessed Advent Morning" in the school's little assembly hall. In every window appeared candelabra, some in the form of Christmas elves, who held the candles in their hands; these were the products of previous classes in handicrafts. Because of the low ceilings, the multitude of candles caused the temperature in the rooms to rise; the cheeks of the children were as red as Christmas apples. Their eyes glistened. There was no doubt about it—Christmas was not far away.

On the second Sunday in Advent, early in the morning, Jon lay in bed listening to the bells from Saint Katarina's Church. It was almost totally dark in the room except for a small shaft of light that crept in between the windowpane and the shade, but this was enough to signify the arrival of a new day.

Jon could hear Mari moving around in the drawing room, setting down the woodbox with a thud and opening the damper with a little click. Had he been listening attentively enough, he might have caught the sounds of the crackles and pops as the first pieces of kindling caught fire.

Jon noticed that it was cold in the room. The warmth of his bed felt wonderful. And today he was free—no scalding hot chocolate to swallow in a frantic rush, no long shivering cold walk up the icy slopes of Three Hill Lane, no unpleasant crowding around the coat hooks and the galoshes in the corridors at school.

On Sunday mornings he was allowed to sleep as long as he wanted, and for the most part he went back to sleep even after Mari came in and lit the fire in his room.

Myriads of small sounds woke him from time to time— Mari puttering around in an adjacent room; Little Brother crying in the nursery; a dove cooing outside the window —but these merely intensified his feeling of well-being, his consciousness that the outside world asked nothing of him.

There were times when he even went back to sleep after Mari had brought in a tray with a coffee cup and a breadbasket and set it on the nightstand beside his bed. But today his stomach was growling, and he peeped at the contents of the breadbasket, which was illuminated by the glow of the fire.

Buttered biscuits, gingersnaps, the first gingerbread men of the season, with currants for eyes, wedges of Advent coffee cake with sugar and almonds on top—now this was a sight for sore eyes! This would beat sleeping and being warm any old time. Jon sat up. He had on a white nightshirt with red trimming, and he was careful not to spill a drop. Mari didn't care for chocolate spots on clothing.

He had just about emptied the breadbasket—only a couple of biscuits were left—and was preparing to pull the covers over his head once more when a whole series of unusual noises disrupted the Sunday calm.

A booming bass voice could be heard from the hallway; it rose and fell, and in the pauses you could almost imagine what Mari's answers were. It turned out to be a pretty long conversation. Jon lay down and stretched out his legs, but he did not cover his head with the blankets. A good bit depended on the outcome of the conversation in the hallway, and Jon listened intently. Of course, some sort of ailment was involved, and Mari tried in her usual tactful way to remind the messenger that this was the doctor's only morning to rest, the only day on which he didn't have to open his office at seven o'clock.

After a few minutes, he could tell that Mari had given in. Her footsteps could be heard as they crossed the linoleum rug in the serving pantry. The outer door had not closed again. The messenger was waiting.

At that point the events followed the old, familiar pattern. Father's voice from the bedroom, a shrill cry of protest from Little Brother, whose feeding time had been interrupted, Mother's and Mari's plaintive voices, while Father no doubt was deciding that he himself would have to speak with the messenger.

The conversation was not long. The outer door was closed following the departure of the visitor, and a few minutes later the kitchen door slammed. It was no trouble for Jon to figure out the sequence of events from the sounds. Father had said, "All right, I'll come, just as quickly as I can," and now Mari was scurrying, a shawl over her shoulders, out to the stonemason's to alert the stable boys about Figaro and the sleigh.

Things were taking place in the bedroom, too. Closet doors and bathroom doors were opened and closed. Little Brother whimpered threateningly for a little while and then began to scream at the top of his lungs for two uninterrupted minutes. Doubtless Mother had been forced to leave him on his own while she attended to Father's various needs.

Jon threw the covers off. The floor was like ice as he dashed barefoot to the washbasin. The big-bellied water jug, with its delightful pattern of pink roses and green leaves, was heavy to lift. The water sloshed out over the sides of the basin.

He knew he had no longer than ten minutes. That was the exact amount of time Father needed to get dressed, check the contents of his bag, which was always packed and ready to go, and fill in any other necessary items.

As Jon stood with his head in the washbasin, the door to his room opened, and Father's voice said, "Good thing you're up. You can come along. But put on plenty of warm clothing. It's way below zero."

"Mmmmm," Jon said, stamping his feet to get a little circulation going in them.

Almost to the split second, both he and Soren and Father were ready. There was a hint of military precision in the well-rehearsed, careful plan of operation.

Mari waved good-by to them from the porch. Mother was nowhere to be seen. It was a sure thing that she was totally occupied calming Little Brother down after the break in the routine.

Because of his frantic hurrying, Jon was wide awake now and quite warm. The hot chocolate had done its work, too. And the sleigh was well enough equipped so that its passengers didn't have to freeze. Besides the carriage apron, which had been borrowed from the gig, there were two sheepskin comforters lined with red-and-green-striped homespun, which covered both the floor and the seats. Jon and Father sat on velvet cushions. Across the width of the sleigh, reaching from side to side, was a huge long-haired jackal skin, grayish yellow in color with light streaks across the back part and tufts of hair standing straight up at the seam joints.

How the jackal skin had ever landed in this corner of the world was a complete mystery, but Father had gotten his hands on it at a public auction.

"This call we're going to make concerns a rather pitiful

story," Father said, giving Soren a salute as the sleigh progressed along by the side of the house. "It doesn't sound good—not good at all."

For a couple of moments, he was silent as he put on his heavy gloves. Figaro's sleigh bells, which up to this time had merely been a few isolated jingles, now sounded evenly and rhythmically. Jon was eager to hear more. He was deeply interested, aware that they were off on a long journey and that the frantic rush the sick call had occasioned was clearly something quite out of the ordinary.

"It was the dairyman from Uddesund who came with the message," Father went on, "and the man who is sick is old Per-Anders out on Kalv Island."

"Is he the one who carves all those wooden figures?" Jon asked.

"Yes, he's the one who whittles the figures—some of them are quite amusing, but some of them are downright macabre. Sometimes they're on sale at the open market."

"What does macabre mean?"

"Well, I guess the best way to describe it is as a sort of grim humor on the subject of sickness and death. When you first look at Per-Anders' figures, they look comical and amusing, but when you examine them a little more closely, you discover that there is something grisly about them—the surfaces are all distorted. . . . But he's very clever with his hands, Per-Anders, and for that matter he's pretty much a jack of all trades. He has had several poems published in the local paper, and he's even published a book that attracted a certain amount of attention among the critics.

"Well, anyway, he lives all alone out there on Kalv Island, where he raises chickens and tends his orchard. At least two times a week, he rows over to the dairy farm with eggs, and in the summer with vegetables, fruit, and berries, and he leaves them with the dairyman, who then sells them in the city. The dairyman or one of his children comes into the city every single day all year long."

Jon nodded. Many times he had seen the dairyman's wagon. It frequently came to deliver cooking fat, grade-A milk, potatoes, and fresh berries to the doctor's house.

"It seems he hadn't seen Per-Anders all week long; he still hadn't shown up by Saturday, and since the dairyman couldn't see any sign of life out on the island, his eldest son rowed over. People are very good to each other out there in the rural areas."

Hitting a couple of ruts, the sleigh skidded as they turned from the Fish Market onto Quarry Road. There was a great screech as it bumped into a sidewalk hidden by the snow.

"Everyone's asleep," Father remarked, casting a glance at the roadway completely empty of people and the gloomy rows of dilapidated sheds and fences.

"Well, to make a long story short, the son had to climb in the kitchen window because the outside door was locked, and he found Per-Anders in bed. The old man was very weak and bilious and complained of terrible pains in his stomach. Naturally, the boy couldn't do anything more than get a fire going in the stove and in the fireplace in the room where the old man was. So when the dairyman came into Soltuna this morning, he thought it would be a good thing to discuss the matter with me. He was afraid the old man would just lie there and die. And he didn't dare move him, either, 'dead weight and sick as he was,' as the dairyman expressed it."

"What do you think it can be, Father?"

Father put the brim of his hat down over his forehead and ears, advising Jon to do the same because the cold made their cheeks sting.

"It's a little hard to say," he said at length, after giving the matter some thought. "I'll have to examine Per-Anders before I can tell. But if it's a question of appendicitis or something of the sort, which would demand an operation, we're in for a very tricky situation. It would be almost impossible to get Per-Anders into a rowboat and then onto the sleigh. It's a terrible thing to be sick when you live on an island so far from anything else and when it's so difficult, because of the miserable roads, to get to the nearest hospital."

"Is it a long way out to the island?"

"Several miles, I'd guess. We're just lucky that Vidar Bay—the little cove off Vidar Lake near Uddesund—is not frozen over yet. There are certain times of year, spring and fall usually, when it's frozen over but the ice won't hold, and then it's utterly impossible to get to Kalv Island.

"Look, Jon—over there on the other side of the street. That's someone you know, isn't it?"

Jon, who had been sitting there idly following one of the stripes on the jackal skin with his thumb as he listened to Father's account, looked up hastily. At a crossroad that the sleigh had just passed stood a solitary gangly figure with his shoulders hunched and his hands in the pockets of a checkered jacket. The boy was the only human being in sight, and you would have thought he might have at least noticed the green sleigh as it passed—the only moving thing in the entire frozen panorama. But he didn't even look up. His back was turned to the street, and he was kicking a piece of ice through the air. It flew over the sidewalk and broke as it hit a fence post.

"Yes, that's Rickard," Jon said, turning his head in the opposite direction. He knew that Rickard had recognized the doctor's sleigh but that he was too shy to wave.

"I thought so," Father said. "All those Svenssons stand the same way—as if they were on the captain's bridge of a ship."

At that very moment, he did something that caused Jon to grasp at the jackal skin in fright. He held Figaro back—Figaro had been going along at a pretty good pace—and stopped the sleigh so suddenly that it skidded off to one side.

"Hello there!" Father cried in a powerful voice. "Don't you recognize us?"

Figaro turned his head. He wanted to know what this was all about. Father lashed the whip through the air instead of waving.

It was no longer possible for the solitary boy to pretend that he hadn't noticed anything. He took a couple of hesitant steps across a pile of dirty snow and slowly climbed over the muddy drifts at the side of the road, finally approaching the sleigh.

Jon pressed himself flat against the back cushion. He longed to pull the jackal skin over his head, wishing desperately that he could simply disappear. He gave his father a dirty look—Father who just sat there so tall and sure of himself in his driving coat and tall hat!

Didn't Father realize that Rickard didn't want any part of this . . . that Jon didn't want any part of this?

Father must have been aware of Jon's glance, but he acted as if nothing had happened.

With slow steps Rickard made his way to the sleigh. His

hands were still deep in his pockets, and he seemed to be having a hard time guiding his feet. He slipped and slid in the
deep ruts.

At last the boy in the checkered jacket came up alongside the sleigh. Stubbornly, Jon stared at the jacket. Mother
had been right about the "poor quality" and "just junk."

The jacket wasn't very old at all, but on close examination, the material had already begun to look sleazy and worn out. The checkered pattern of the cloth had almost disappeared. Where were the yellows and rusts that in the beginning had looked so dashing? Or was it just that the jacket looked so unattractive because of the cold, gray, unappealing winter day?

"Good morning! Your name is Rickard, isn't it?"

"How terrible! How unthinkable that Father would speak to Rickard in this fashion," Jon thought. To be sure, he and Jon knew one another, but that was in school! Couldn't Father fathom the fact that Rickard surely didn't want to have anything to do with people who wore fur-trimmed coats and rode around in sleighs, unless he were absolutely forced to? Jon couldn't bring himself to look Rickard in the eye. Never more would he even want to see his face. Now there would be even further reasons for envy, jealousy, and contempt.

Jon continued to stare at the jacket. He concentrated on one of its black buttons. He wasn't going to take any risk. Not for anything in the world would he have Rickard think he had had anything to do with this incident.

Luckily, Father asked nothing of Jon. Briskly, amiably, he said, "I believe you and Jon are classmates, right? I remember hearing this somewhere. We're on our way out into the country to make a sick call. Would you like to ride along? Soltuna doesn't seem to be too lively on Sundays!"

Jon's cheeks were as hot as fire. The heat spread to his forehead, his throat, throughout his entire body. How could Father do a thing like this? How *could* he?

Rickard cleared his throat.

"No," he said, and Jon, considering the frame of mind he himself was in, was surprised that the boy's voice sounded no different than it usually did. "No, there's not much going on around here!"

"Well, hop up!" Father said. "It wouldn't surprise me at all if the sun came out, and we might have a very pleasant ride. Move over, Jon, and make room for Rickard. You're both as thin as pencils, so there's plenty of space. Creep in under the cover and you won't be so cold. Shall we stop at your house so that you can find out if it's all right for you to go along, or at least tell your parents so they won't be concerned?"

Rickard had stamped the snow and ice off his worn-out boots. A good portion of his legs was exposed between the top of the boots and the bottom of his pants. Rickard was wearing gray woolen socks. Apparently he wasn't afraid of material that caused your skin to itch—not Rickard.

His answer to Father's question took the form of a shrug of the shoulders.

"That won't be necessary. There's no one who cares where I am. Anyhow, Mother's at the hotel helping out today."

In answer to Father's signal, Figaro took off with such a jerk that all three of them swung off to one side of the seat. Once more the merry jingle of the sleigh bells could be heard. There was something ethereal about their sound—it was as if they wanted to help the human race forget about everything trivial, everything gray, everything unpleasant.

"Ride with us," they seemed to be saying. "Don't concentrate on the dirty snow in the gutters, on the murky swamps, on the stripped landscape by the quarry! Forget about suspiciousness and jealousy! Play with us! Listen to us instead!"

NINE

It would be hard to tell whether it was thanks to the sleigh bells, to Father, or to the warm sun that finally came out. In any event, Jon's anxiety and shyness disappeared little by little. Later, when he thought back on the sleigh ride, he couldn't understand what had paralyzed him so completely at first. Nothing extraordinary had happened. Father had merely asked Rickard, who was standing on a street corner obviously bored, to ride along with them on their Sunday journey, and Rickard, after the first few moments of confusion and uncertainty, had found the sleigh ride much to his liking. He couldn't conceal his enjoyment. He pulled his cap down over his ears, and Father handed him a jar of Vaseline and told him to rub some on his cheeks, his neck, and his nose to prevent chapping. He laughed out loud frequently and displayed a lively curiosity about things in general.

"Where are we off to? What if Per-Anders dies before we get there? Is it true what people say—that he whittles his birchwood figures with an ordinary penknife?"

Father answered the queries patiently, and Jon could tell by his tone of voice that he thought Rickard was amusing and very nice to talk to. Father was not the sort who pretended—not even to make another person happy.

Jon suddenly found himself entering the conversation. He told Rickard all about the small horses at the quarry shaft, about the fact that they often had to pull loads that were too heavy for them and that occasionally they were struck down by blasting in the mine because no one had bothered to get them out of the way. He discovered that Rickard was just as moved as he had been when he first heard about the horses.

Rickard wanted to know if there wasn't some protection for the undersized horses. Wasn't there some law covering them?

Father said that he had already spoken to the veterinarian in the district and that he would speak to him again about them.

"There are many things that are not as they should be," said Father. "And it's not right at all to see these things and stand around doing nothing. You have to raise opposition, and you have to keep doing it again and again. It pays to keep harping on something like that."

Both of the boys were pleased at Father's statement. Rickard said he thought it was terrible when animals were mistreated. After all, they couldn't speak up or defend themselves. They just had to suffer. People could cry out for help; they could complain. Being unkind to an animal was the very worst thing of all. It was cowardly.

Gradually, Father lapsed into silence, and the boys carried on a lively conversation. When you came right down to it, there were thousands of subjects to discuss. They both expressed annoyance at one particular teacher at school;

they had both carved their initials on their desks, though this was strictly forbidden. Rickard asked how Pixie's puppies were and said that Pixie herself was fine and that every now and then he took her out for a walk.

The journey to Uddesund was as rapid and as merry as the jingle of the bells. They passed a stretch of pine woods where the soft white snow still clung to the branches, which were bent down to the ground. They looked like crinolines on elegant ladies.

"Wouldn't it be fun to be an elf," Jon said suddenly, "and ski from the top to the bottom of a tree like that? To jump from branch to branch? You could really work up some speed!"

As soon as the words were out of his mouth, he was sorry. He must have sounded dreadfully childish. He and Father often shared little private jokes of this sort during their trips. Father was fond of fairy tales and stories about elves, wood sprites, dwarfs, and trolls. It was easy to see how these fantasies had come about when you watched the fog lift on an autumn evening, when you saw storm-tossed trees on the deserted hills. Being alone—in really wild country—was something Father and Jon were used to because of their trips, and they knew how wild ideas and strange thoughts could creep into their minds.

But Rickard came from the slums. Surely he would think that Jon should have passed the age where he was concerned with trolls and elves.

Jon lapsed into an anxious silence. Feverishly, he searched for another subject to bring up, but as usual on such occasions, his brain went dead. He couldn't think of a thing.

At that moment Rickard said thoughtfully, "You know,

you're right. Pine-tree branches are like ski slopes where you have to take a lot of jumps. You're clever at expressing yourself. You use words descriptively. . . ."

Turning to Father, he said unexpectedly, "There's nobody in class who can write better compositions than Jon."

Father had to laugh.

"Is that so? I didn't know that. But he's had a chance to see a good deal of life, both in the city and out here in the country. He never tells us much about school, our Jon. But I can tell you, Rickard, I've heard a good bit about how good you are in school!"

"Ahhhh," Rickard said, happily embarrassed.

Down toward Uddesund the hills were stonier and terribly steep, so steep that at times they all felt as if Figaro's back and long black tail were directly below them and that at any moment the sleigh was going to fall on top of him. It was a strange sensation, and both Jon and Rickard braced themselves by pressing their feet against the uneven floor of the sleigh. In addition, the road was rough and icy, which often made the sleigh scrape against the piles of snow at the sides and the passengers bump against one another. At one point they had to go off the road to avoid a fallen tree trunk. Figaro was very cautious in negotiating the road bank.

Finally, the woods thinned out, and they could see before them the blue shiny water of the cove. Snow-covered stubble fields stretched out on both sides of the road, and at the bottom of the slope itself were the cottages of Uddesund, red with white trimmings. Stone walls, built when the land had been cleared, formed the borders of the fields and stretched to where the cowsheds, stables, storehouses, and coach houses stood. High juniper bushes, like guards on parade, formed hedges around the houses, and there were rows of them along the road leading down to the water.

The dairyman came hurrying to meet them. One of his sons took care of Figaro, who was to be left in their stable.

All three of the travelers were a little stiff in the fingers and cold after their long sleigh trip, but there was no time to warm themselves in the cottage, although the dairyman invited them to step inside. Father wasn't still for a second; grabbing his bag, he rushed alongside the juniper hedge down the steep, winding path to the water. The dairyman, clearly not accustomed to such frantic haste, had a hard time keeping up with him, and Rickard and Jon ran behind them, shivering in the penetrating cold.

The pier was made of a single plank laid out on stones. A gray skiff, properly cared for but well used, had been dragged up on the shore nearby. It seemed strange to see it there with snowdrifts almost covering its square stern and with icicles hanging from the oars. To Jon, a skiff was something associated with the green of the summer and lazy holidays. Along the shoreline the water had frozen, but out a small distance in the cove, between the mainland and Kalv Island, which from a distance looked like a rounded, wooded hill, the waves, white-topped and foaming, danced as if they wanted to make the most of the little bit of freedom still left before the heavy winter shackled them completely.

"Up there is Per-Anders' place," the dairyman said, pointing. "Hold a straight course over the water, Doctor; you can see that yellow spot right over there, can't you? Well, when you get closer, you'll see that it divides into two arms, and all you have to do is row into the opening. There's a small dock and then an old washhouse and then you're there.

Thank God you could come, Doctor. Mother was over a while ago, and she says he's in pretty bad shape. Doctor, do you think you'll need any help?"

"Well, I have the boys with me," Father said as he put his bag on the forward thwart. "I think they can give me all the help I'll need. Thanks for offering, but the fewer in the boat, the faster we can row. Good-by. We'll see you later."

All the while he was talking, he was pushing the boat into the water and motioning to the boys to take their places in the stern. He moved with a speed and agility that was astonishing when you considered the voluminous driving coat he was wearing.

"Shall I row?" Jon asked.

"No, better let me row over," Father said, "and you and Rickard can be responsible for the trip back."

The dairyman gave the skiff a shove, and Father, with a couple of mighty pulls on the oars, got them headed in the right direction. But Rickard, who hadn't had time to sit down, stumbled on the frost-covered thwart and fell on Jon. By the time they had gotten themselves straightened out, the little boat was moving through the blue water—appearing even bluer because of the whiteness of the shore. There were gusts of wind. They could see the black crags and the belt of yellowish reeds surrounding Kalv Island; with each passing minute, the reeds seemed to occupy a broader space.

"I don't know how to row. Do you?" Rickard asked softly.

"Yes, I do. I learned in the summers out in the country."

"Oh, do you have another home?"

There was a momentary pause, during which Jon began

to realize that Rickard lived the year around in Soltuna on Quarry Road. The ninety long summer days, which to Jon meant living another kind of life entirely in the family's summer cottage on a cape in Vidar Lake, meant to Rickard nothing but dry streets and, perhaps at the most, open windows. No doubt he could go barefoot, but there were thistles, nettles, and weeds on the overgrown lots at the edge of the city. Jon recalled that this was their "summer playground."

"Yes," he said a little doubtfully. "We have a summer place."

"Do you have a boat there?"

"Yes, a skiff. Just about like this one."

"Is it the same color?"

"No, ours is green and white."

Jon turned his head away. He wished so much that he could stick his hands in the water that was coursing and bubbling past them. But all he could do was to sit with his hands clasped in his lap, clumsy as they were in huge woolly mittens.

The skiff that he rowed every summer was white and green, as he had told Rickard. The grass was green; the summer skies were blue; there were white clouds, a red house, yellow rambler roses, sky-blue curtains in his little bedroom beneath the eaves. The eaves themselves were black. The summer was a wide expanse of colors to play in, to be alternately warm and cool in, to sleep in, to wake in.

"I've only been out in the country once before," Rickard said.

"Where was that?"

"Well, the Salvation Army arranged an excursion last summer out to Vidinge. There was an orchestra there, and they played and sang."

Jon kept quiet. Glancing at Father out of the corner of his eye, he could tell that he was listening, in spite of the fact that the boys were talking in low voices—almost as if they were exchanging secrets.

"But there were so many people there that time—old ones and young ones—that you didn't get to enjoy much peace

124

and quiet," Rickard added. "I love it in the country, but when I'm in the country, I want to be left alone."

Just before they reached the little sheltered bay that served Kalv Island, the skiff hit the waves sideways, and the boat began to rock. Rickard held on with both hands. It was fairly obvious that he wasn't used to water and boats. Maybe he had never sat in a boat before!

The gap in the reeds was narrow, and the stiff stalks scraped against the sides of the boat with a rustling sound. A duck flew down and landed only inches from the boat.

They had arrived. Climbing over Father, Jon hopped up when they reached the dock. There was a chain fastened to the bow of the skiff, and Father directed Jon to tie them up properly.

"I'll go right on up. Come along as soon as you can!" he said.

Before Jon's icy fingers could get the chain wound around one of the pilings on the dock, Father was already halfway up the small path to Per-Anders' cottage.

Very curious, the boys took a look around. A skiff, pretty much like the one they had come in, had been pulled ashore down by the washhouse, which was badly in need of repair. A couple of boxes, in the bottom of which fish scales glistened, stood against the wall. Four or five nets hung drying on a simple wooden rack, and inside the door they could make out piles of homemade crayfish traps.

"He's a fisherman!" Jon remarked.

"And there are his chickens!" Rickard cried eagerly. "Hey, can't we go and take a look at them?"

They could hear the hens cackling from a shed just up

the hill. Rickard led the way. It was evident that chickens were something unusual to him—out and out sensational. A number of brown and white hens, pecking grains of corn and clucking, crowded into the corner of a small enclosure.

"I wonder if they've had anything to eat since the old man got sick," Jon said as he surveyed the situation.

"Does he live here all alone?" Rickard wondered aloud. "But what if he were to fall down and break his leg or something like that? If it were to happen outside, he might just lie there and freeze to death."

Jon nodded.

"Father says he's crazy to live out here all alone when he's so old. . . . It looks to me as if the dairyman's wife gave the hens something to eat, but we'll have to look after them again before we leave. Come on. There are probably lots of things we'll have to help with up there."

They climbed higher up the slope. Like most of the houses in that area, Per-Anders' cottage was painted red. In the background were gray aspens and white-trunked birches. Out in front was an orchard with old, gnarled apple trees, a potato field, strawberry barrels, and raspberry bushes. There were even some hotbeds, the glass panes of which gleamed in the morning light. There was less snow here than on the mainland. Here it was like a light, dry powder over the landscape.

Rickard turned around. Below them glistened the blue bay with its wreath of reeds. On the other side of the cove, you could see Uddesund's red cottages nestled on the snow-covered hills.

"It's beautiful here!" he said. "And so quiet!"

They stepped up into Per-Anders' closed-in porch. It

was small, with linoleum covering the floor, two Windsor chairs, and a table with an oilcloth covering. In the windows were fuchsias and begonia plants. An array of flowerpots and boxes of black soil containing tender shoots gave witness to the fact that Per-Anders used his porch as a hothouse.

With one finger Jon dug into one of the pots.

"We've got to water these. They'll all die otherwise. But I think it's best if we go inside first and see what's going on."

From the porch they entered the kitchen; the walls were blue, and on the shelves above the stove were shiny copper pots. The stove with its four cast-iron lids looked very black and cold. To the boys who had just come in from the below-zero temperature, the kitchen seemed warm and cozy, but Jon realized, from seeing the frostbitten leaves in the flowerpots, that the temperature inside the cottage was anything but high.

It was a low-ceilinged room. Both Rickard and Jon could touch the ceiling with their fingertips. From an adjoining room, Father's voice could be heard distinctly. He was asking questions—that was easy to tell—but if he received any answers, they were impossible to catch.

"Per-Anders, of course, is very handy with everything and anything, isn't he?" Rickard half whispered. "Don't you think so? Considering that he's an old man out here alone—no mother, no wife, or anything?"

Jon had to agree.

"Yes, he's very clever—you know that the minute you see his wooden figures. But it's not easy to take care of a place like this. All those chickens, and the garden, and fishing—and then he has to row over to the mainland or walk across the ice in the wintertime quite often. A big job like repairing the cottage roof would be hard for him to do all by himself. You can tell by the condition of the washhouse. He's not a very big man, and he doesn't look very strong."

"Oh, I know. I've seen him. But this would be a wonderful life, I think, don't you? To be left in peace and quiet and to do just as you please."

This was the second time Rickard had brought up the subject of being "left in peace and quiet." This was, no doubt, very important for someone forced to share small quarters with a large family, for a person who, even outside his home, lived his life among many children.

The low white door to the next room opened. Father had to duck his head as he stepped over the threshold.

Both boys peered curiously through the half-open door. A mumbling noise that turned into sort of a whine could be heard faintly.

"Well," Father said. "Well, I'll have to take a few things off. I'm going to have to give him a thorough examination. Here, Jon, take my heavy coat—and the jacket, too. I've got to be able to move easily, you see."

Jon reached out his arms. He almost disappeared under the pile of Father's heavy clothing.

Father smiled slightly, but it was an absent-minded smile. Tall and thin, he stood there in his white shirt and long dark trousers. His high collar was stiff; he wore a necktie and had starched white cuffs. One by one he removed certain articles from his pockets, but as if deep in thought. These he handed to Rickard.

"Just take everything out to the porch," Father said. "I noticed some hooks to hang coats on."

The boys did as they were told. When they returned to the kitchen, they found Father standing by the stove. He was staring down at an empty water bucket. He stroked his black beard. Then he gripped a wooden handle on a cupboard by the stove and turned it. As he opened the door, he saw a woodbox, empty except for a couple of pieces of bark at the bottom.

"Uh huh," Father said, drumming on the woodbox. "This looks pretty desolate here. . . . Goodness, how deserted. . . . Per-Anders!" he suddenly cried in such a loud voice that Rickard jumped a foot. "Per-Anders, are you thirsty?"

Once again a mumble was heard from inside the room, together with a number of disjointed words . . . "thirsty . . . bottle in the cupboard . . ." All these were followed by a number of local swear words, most of which the boys had heard before.

Rickard glanced awkwardly at the floor. Jon pursed his lips.

But Father laughed, loudly and heartily. "Yes, sir, Per-Anders. Now I *know* you're sick. This is the first time that I've ever heard you swear!"

"The bottle will just have to stay in the cupboard, at least for the time being, I believe. But the boys can certainly go after some water. Right this minute. Here is the bucket. And listen, Jon. We're going to need wood—piles of wood. Lots and lots of water, too, as far as that's concerned."

"I saw a wood carrier down on the dock."

"Fine. But get going. The well, Per-Anders? . . . Oh, I get it—off to the right on the other side of the small willows."

The boys stumbled out of the door. They were not long

in discovering the path to the well. It was both steep and slippery.

"How in the world are we going to get water up out of that hole?" Rickard asked, looking down between the dark greenish sides suspiciously. "This *is* the well, isn't it?"

"Sure. See, you have to lower a bucket. Use that gadget there," Jon said, pointing at the winch with a rope and an old rusty crank. "Just wait and see—providing this old winch isn't too rusty."

Rickard's eyes filled with admiration as he watched Jon hang a bucket on the hook at the end of the rope. With the winch creaking, the bucket disappeared into the depths of the well. The crank almost danced.

"I guess you've done this before, haven't you?"

"Oh, sure. Almost all the cottages out in the country have wells like this. Listen, Rickard, we should have another bucket. This won't be enough. We can each carry one."

"But the old man can't possibly drink that much water, can he?"

"Oh, no. This is water for washing. Father has to wash himself and the old man, too, and maybe we'll have to sterilize the instruments that Father has to use. Look, run back and see what you can find, please!"

Rickard disappeared in great haste in the direction of the cottage. When he returned with a dented pail in hand, Jon had managed to draw up the first bucket, filled two thirds full. His face was red from the exertion.

Silently, Rickard watched as Jon inspected the new pail critically.

"I'm sure he uses this one for chicken feed—sure as the

dickens," he remarked gloomily. "We'll have to rinse it out first. If we don't, the water will be dirty."

An old worn-out scrub brush, obviously used for similar purposes, lay in the moss. Jon scrubbed and rinsed the pail, using in addition some sand and clean snow. Finally, they managed to fill both pails almost full of water and began the journey back.

Fortunately, carrying the wood turned out to be much simpler. There was a good supply of chopped-up logs in the woodshed close to the cottage. They had to chop some kindling wood themselves, with Jon showing Rickard how to do it.

"All I can say is I hope these things will catch fire," Jon said as he crawled around on all fours on the kitchen floor, poking kindling and pine cones, which he had found in the woodshed, into the stove opening.

"I don't understand how you know just exactly what to do," Rickard said with great respect in his voice.

Jon opened the top damper. He also found a second ventilator. Drops of perspiration gathered on his forehead, and he managed to get a splinter in his finger. Crouching on his heels, he savored the delicious moment when the fire caught and began to blaze beneath the stove lids.

"Well, I've done this a good many times," he said a little absent-mindedly—the way many people do after making great but successful efforts. "It's kind of tricky at times, but this stove is a good one, and he has kept it in good condition. You should see what happens deeper in the woods where nobody but the timber cutters live. When Father is called to one of their shacks to disinfect wounds, take stitches,

or bandage up injuries, it's almost hopeless. It takes forever just to get the water boiling. And the water simply has to be boiled because that is what kills the bacteria; that's what makes it possible to use the water. Otherwise, there can be infection, gangrene can set in, and I don't know what else."

Rickard observed Jon's hands, which had always given the impression of being weak and uncertain as he used them on the bars and ladders in the gym. They were not much better when it came to writing or printing. Rickard had been accustomed to looking at them with a sort of idle contempt, had even thought to himself that they resembled girls' hands. To be truthful, he hadn't always kept his observation to himself. He had mentioned the fact to some of his best friends and admirers among the strong, aggressive boys in the class.

Rickard blushed as he recalled this. By now there was a good fire in Per-Anders' stove, and the sparks were flying. Using the lifter, Jon removed a couple of the stove lids. He put a huge kettle of water on the larger hole and the coffee-pot on the other.

"Jon," Father called from the next room. "How is everything coming along?"

"Everything is under way. But it will be quite a while before the water boils, of course."

"All right. Come on in; I want to talk to you."

Rickard followed Jon into the room. Both of them stopped, somewhat frightened, right at the door. The peculiar smell coming from the neglected sick man hit them both. This was nothing new for Jon, who had experienced the same smells in low-lying gray cottages or in chilly furnished rooms in the city, but he was not prepared to see the old man on the sofa over in the corner looking so hollow-eyed and ashen. His thin body resembled a stick beneath the gray blanket. There were no sheets. Clearly there had been some sort of accident, for the sheets were piled on the floor over by the wall.

Apart from the deplorable condition that both the old man and his bed were in, the remainder of the room was something you would scarcely have expected in what, from the outside, looked like a simple fisherman's cottage. Bright-colored rag rugs covered the well-scrubbed floor. The faint winter sun peeped in through blue-and-white-striped curtains, illuminating Per-Anders' enormous workbench, which stood beside one of the three windows. Half-finished figures, pieces of wood, and a small knotty birch log lay on its chipped surface, together with knives of all sizes, chisels, and other tools. It looked as if the person who had been working there had had to drop everything just when he was busiest.

In the middle of the room was a round table with an Oriental-looking cloth covering that reached almost to the floor. Jon remembered hearing that Per-Anders had gone to sea when he was much younger. The white-painted clock, which stood in the corner, had a wide face and highly ornamented hands. A cupboard decorated in bright colors, reaching from floor to ceiling, bore the date 1702.

There were copper candlesticks with handles in one window and low-footed copper molds in the other. Between the two windows on the long side of the room, opposite the workbench, was a bookcase crowded with books. The overflow was piled up on the floor. Two dignified ceramic dogs— white with black spots—brightened up the shelf on a white ceramic stove that stood against the other side of the wall from the kitchen stove.

Rickard felt that he had never before seen such a beautiful room. The school principal's awe-inspiring, high-ceilinged reception room with its velvet draperies and overstuffed chairs, which up to this time had struck him as the height of luxury, was nothing compared to this.

Jon's mouth had dropped open in astonishment. He began to think. He had seen and heard more in his lifetime than had

Rickard, and he could form impressions more surely, more clearly.

With great seriousness and respect, he looked at the bird-like gray-bearded face leaning back on the pillow. Jon realized that the old man had created a very lively atmosphere in his small cottage, in spite of the barrenness of the island; this was a cultivated home, but the old man hadn't copied the habits and tastes of others. This was no chilly, uninviting bachelor's den; neither was it a room that looked as if it had been planned down to the minutest detail by a professional decorator. Per-Anders' cottage was alive—just as his wooden figures were.

It was terrible that he was sick in bed now, sick and helpless, watching his possessions, which were so much a part of him, lying unused and uncared for.

The fact that Per-Anders was terribly sick was evident to Jon long before Father began to talk. He could tell it from Father's voice as well—calm, almost nonchalant though it was—as he spoke from the chair near the sofa. It was no doubt a comfort to Father to think that he could fool both Per-Anders and Rickard!

"The only thing wrong with Per-Anders is that he has an inflamed appendix," Father said curtly, getting right to the heart of the matter. "And now we're going to have to lay out our plans. Naturally, the best thing would be to get him to the nearest hospital immediately and on the operating table. But that would take at least a couple of hours—it's a long distance to cover. And during the trip, he would be joggled and shaken, and that would probably cause his appendix to rupture."

Father paused a moment, putting his hand on the elevated

ridge formed by Per-Anders' legs. In silence, Jon filled in the pause for himself: ". . . if it hasn't ruptured already that is."

"Therefore," Father said, fastening his kind eyes on the old man's pale face, as if he wanted to offer him the comfort every good doctor ought to carry around with him in his bag, "therefore, I have decided to operate right here and now, just as quickly as possible."

Jon noticed that the form beneath the blankets changed. It seemed to become straighter and more angular. Poor Per-Anders . . . he must be trying to protect himself from the inevitable!

"But you've got nothing to fear, Per-Anders," Father continued immediately. "I'm absolutely positive that everything is going to be all right. Maybe you won't believe it, but I've removed a good many appendixes in my day—at the hospital, of course—but with the boys' help, we'll make everything as clean and sanitary around here as it would be in any hospital. I can't honestly tell you it's going to be pleasant. I won't try to bluff you—it's going to hurt. But I have with me a fine new kind of hypodermic, and there's a new type of injection that will help you through the worst of it."

Father turned to Jon, all the while keeping his hand pressed against Per-Anders' leg.

"As soon as the coffee is ready—and put plenty of coffee in so that it will be strong as the dickens—we're going to give Per-Anders a real shot of it. Open the cupboard—wasn't that where you said you kept the bottle, Per-Anders? Oh, yes. Right over there! Oh, and tell me: where do you keep towels and sheets and linen and such?"

"Up there." Per-Anders pointed with his crooked index

finger to the top part of the big cupboard. "Just turn the key, boy!"

There was a slight creak as the cupboard door opened, revealing three shelves painted blue, on which were piles of tablecloths, towels, sheets, and pillowcases—all snow-white except for an occasional red or green border.

Jon became aware that Father knew Per-Anders better than one might have imagined. There weren't many cottages in which he would have dared ask for the linen closet.

"Goodness gracious, these are so lovely that I scarcely dare to use them!"

Father rose to his feet and surveyed the contents of the cupboard. He contradicted himself immediately as he took down a stack of towels.

"The table under the ceiling lamp will be the instrument table," he went on. "Wipe it off, Jon, and put this cloth on it. We'll need a washbasin and all the clean rags there are. Just point, Per-Anders. Don't talk. Boys, you take care of the stove. We'll have to have more water, and you must keep the woodbox full. Get a fire going in the ceramic stove. We still have two hours of daylight before us, but see to it that the kerosene lamp is filled. I wonder what the dairyman's wife did when she came over here—just sit at the side of the bed and rock?"

TEN

❄

The half hour that ensued was, for Jon, the most frantic he had ever lived through. He flew between the stove and the room, giving orders to Rickard and, in turn, taking orders from Father. He had removed his heavy boots out on the porch, and Rickard, who had fulfilled his responsibilities where the wood and water were concerned, followed his example. Thus, into plain view came his stocking feet—covered by the remnants of a pair of socks that would have caused Mother and Mari to faint at the sight of them. But the atmosphere that dismal Sunday in the workroom of Per-Anders' cottage was such that his worn-out socks caused no shyness on Rickard's part nor shocked surprise on the part of the others. Everyone noticed, but nothing further was made of it.

Rickard's toes, which had attained their full freedom, were red from the cold but otherwise scrupulously clean. Both he and Jon had to scrub their hands and nails with scalding hot water, disinfectant, and soap, using a nail brush that was part of the equipment in the doctor's bag. Jon was amazed that Father examined even Rickard's nails so minutely. He was aware that he himself might have to handle some of the sterilized cloths and perhaps some of the instruments, but Father didn't have to be so fussy about Rickard, who was going to take care of the stove, the fire, and other lesser tasks.

Jon was blissfully ignorant of the fact that Father, in all seriousness, figured that Jon, who would have to witness most of the operation, might possibly faint.

Father even carried his plans so far that, under the pretext of a cup of coffee to fortify himself, he managed to catch a moment alone with Rickard out by the stove while Jon was carrying the coffee with a shot of whisky in it to Per-Anders' bedside.

"Listen carefully," Father said in great haste and brevity to Rickard. "It strikes me that you're a sensible boy who won't lose his head in an emergency. Jon is used to helping me with a lot of simple tasks, and he's going to be my assistant during the operation. But he's never seen anything like this before. It is dimly possible—just possible, you understand, since you never know how people are going to react to things of this sort—that he might get sick, in which case you'd have to rush in and be my helper. In that event, see to it that you get Jon into the other room. There's a little bedroom off to the side of the other room, with a little sofa where he can rest. You must keep your hands hospital clean and do exactly as I say!"

Father gave Rickard a pat on the back, and Rickard followed Father's admonitions by once more filling the washbasin by the stove with bubbling-hot water and beginning to wash his hands.

Inside the workroom the blankets had been removed from the sofa. Rickard had taken them outside and hung them up to air. The soiled sheets had been put to soak in a huge copper kettle.

Per-Anders himself lay on a mattress, which had been covered with a clean white sheet and placed on the sofa. He had emptied the coffee cup in one swallow. Jon was astonished that Father had made him drink coffee with whisky in it. He had never known his father to express anything but contempt for alcohol, no matter for what purpose.

A little color had returned to Per-Anders' sunken cheeks. It was obvious that he didn't "take to the bottle" very often; the bottle was almost full. He appeared to be sleepy; he seemed relaxed. Father watched him out of the corner of one eye.

On the table beneath the ceiling lamp, the instruments were laid out—the hypodermic that Father had mentioned, pincers, tongs, and some small shiny clamps, which Father pointed out to Jon.

"If I ask for nippers, these are what I want you to hand me. You must pick them up with the tongs—this way."

In addition, on the table were a couple of objects that resembled narrow razor blades with steel handles, short pieces of thin thread, piles of compresses, a crock, and some of Per-Anders' own porcelain bowls, three of them in all, which with their hand-painted flowers looked unnaturally cheerful and gay in the setting in which they had landed.

Jon began to think that Father had been prepared for this eventuality—that he had been ready for the possibility of an operation. Generally, he didn't carry along so much equipment in his bag. Jon also noticed that Father stayed between the patient and the instrument table after the instruments had been laid out. Per-Anders, now minus his pillow, couldn't see the arrangement on the table, and Jon felt that this was a good thing.

Father showed Jon precisely where to stand.

"Here, right behind me, close to the table. Don't come any closer. If there's something I can't reach myself, I'll tell you. Do you know what I mean by tampons? Well, if both my hands are occupied, it might be necessary for you to step a little closer, but otherwise stay right where you are."

Rickard leaned against the door leading to the kitchen. He was wide-eyed and a little pale around his nose, Jon thought.

And what did he himself look like, he wondered. He felt somewhat trembly inside. He had been ordered to roll his sweater and shirtsleeves above his elbows, and it was so cold that he had gooseflesh, though by now it was warmer in the room than it had been.

Father's movements grew more rapid. He was certainly not pale. His appearance was as usual while he talked cheerfully to Per-Anders, who had a clean, white nightshirt on. From his position Jon could see Per-Anders' head, his gray hair, and his gray stubby beard. The old man's eyes were clear, and he looked extraordinarily collected.

Cautiously, Father listened to Per-Anders' heartbeat through the stethoscope. By Father's movements Jon could judge that he had filled the hypodermic needle and had given the patient a shot in the thigh.

Once more Father spoke to Per-Anders.

"When it's all over, you'll see that you're going to recover much more quickly than you imagine. And we'll arrange for you to have some company tonight. You'll be far from comfortable after the operation, and you'll have to count on being in bed at least a week or so until the incision heals. Tomorrow I'll come out and take a look at you . . ."

Father's speech became slower and slower. At length he was silent altogether. Per-Anders didn't seem to be moving at all. At this point, Father began to move even faster than before. Jon, wondering what was going on, craned his neck to see. Father leaned over Per-Anders' feet.

Jon had to swallow a couple of times. He realized that Father was tying down the patient's legs. Jon had noticed a small rope and had wondered what it was going to be used for.

This was a fairly normal procedure, because it would never do to have the patient, consciously or unconsciously, begin to kick. But for the first time, Jon felt not only uneasy and excited but also afraid.

This was a pretty chancy venture, the whole thing. Father must have had to make a difficult choice—either to try to cover the long distance to the hospital or to act here and now.

Ether fumes filled the entire room. Father put on the rubber gloves he had taken out of a protective covering. You could see that he was washing the place where the incision would be, after which he threw the used cotton into a wastebasket that had been placed right by the sofa.

Then for a while he bent over the patient. He had the bundle of sterilized cloths handy, and now the ether fumes became even stronger.

The minutes passed. The grandfather clock with its flat, expressionless face ticked on and on. The movements of Father's elbows and back were so small that one wondered if he even had hands.

"Jon! The tampons! Put them on the edge of the sofa here!"

Taking a couple of steps forward with the desired objects in hand, Jon could see, for a brief second, the incision surrounded with a soft framework of towels; he noticed, with a certain horror, that the dark red blood seemed to be coming out in a veritable wave.

He stepped back to his position. His heart was beating wildly, and there was a ringing in his ears. How could Father? How did he dare? If the blood continued to flow, how could he see? Was he truly prepared for what was happening?

He must have been. Nothing about his posture or manner indicated that everything was not as it should be. He stood deeply bowed.

At the same moment when Jon stepped forward with the tampons, Per-Anders' arms moved vehemently. Doubtless he was fairly unconscious, but . . . Jon shut his eyes and gritted his teeth. Per-Anders wasn't out cold. From his sunken lips came a low, wailing moan.

Father mumbled. Actually, he was half humming, which was quite moving. Father couldn't sing at all.

"Quiet, now. Just keep still . . . still . . . it will soon be over . . . over soon . . . !"

But it still took a frightfully long time.

"Reach me the small scissors, Jon!"

"The nippers, Jon! Right here in my hand!"

How wonderful it was just to move! You got dizzy just standing and standing. Or was it maybe the ether?

Oh, good heavens, Per-Anders had begun to move again!

He had raised his head, and he dangled part way across Father's upper arm. There he stayed.

"Father . . . can I do anything?"

"No, stand still. It's all right . . . if I can just . . . get . . ."

Rickard stood on the other side of the table. He whispered hoarsely, "Are you all right, Jon? How do you feel? I thought I saw you . . . sort of . . . swaying . . ."

Jon straightened up. He didn't know he had been unsteady.

It seemed unbelievable that Father could work with Per-Anders' head against his arm. But now . . . now . . . the old man moved again. Oh, thank God . . . he slid back toward the pillow! But just as he did, he coughed, at which point he began to vomit. His whole body shook, and a flood of some sort of murky substance came out of his mouth, streamed across Father's arm and down his shirt.

For a few horrible seconds, Jon imagined that blood wa issuing from the old man's mouth. He was terrified. But onc he caught the smell, he realized that it was nothing wors than ordinary vomiting.

"It doesn't matter," Father said, and his voice sounded a most happy. "Not a bit. Just let it be, Jon. Actually, tl worst is over."

Jon stole a glance toward the kitchen door. Rickard w leaving the room. With great haste, he turned around a disappeared into the kitchen. Half-stifled sounds could heard. Apparently, Rickard didn't feel too well. Of cou it was hardly an attractive sight. To be sure, Per-Anders lying down again, but his beard, his face . . . !

It certainly was far from an appealing vision, but still Jon was not to be scared. He had heard the note of triumph in Father's last words. What did it matter how Per-Anders looked? What difference did it make how he smelled? Not even Per-Anders' moans and groans made much impression. He was alive—he was even conscious, more or less—and everything in time was going to be all right.

A pair of scissors and some pincers fell to the floor.

"How goes it, Jon?"

"Fine, just fine. How is everything with you, Father?"

"Great. I've got it out now—and it was an ugly rascal, too. Green and swollen but not ruptured."

"Can I take a look?"

"Afterwards. Later on. Per-Anders, can you hear me? I know you're sick to your stomach now, of course, but that rascal of an appendix of yours is out. You'll get to take a look at it later on—preserved in a test tube. Are you in pain? Tell me where?"

Father's voice was as mild as if he had been addressing Mother or Little Brother.

He got no reply. Per-Anders' head slid off to one side. His mouth, wreathed by his tousled beard, was wide open. Whether this was because of the pain, the effort, or the great relief, it was hard to say. But now, now that the worst was over, he was truly out cold!

ELEVEN

At the cottage on the shore of Kalv Island, they worked long after dusk fell. The fact that Per-Anders had passed out caused a good bit of commotion. Jon stood at the head of the sofa, anxious and concerned, while Father cold-bloodedly, after having listened to the old man's heartbeat, took advantage of every second to put the final stitches in the incision.

Rickard, white as a sheet, had sneaked up to the table and was whispering excitedly, "Is he dead? Is he dead?"

"Not at all!" Jon said, and Father appended calmly:

"He'll come to again pretty soon!"

And he did. And no celebrity in the world could have been the object of more elation and admiration than he was when he opened his eyes. To begin with, he was somewhat out of his senses, saying a string of unconnected, meaningless phrases, and he was clearly very sick to his stomach. But surprisingly rapidly, the fog lifted for him, and he seemed only a little confused and astonished over what had been accomplished.

After that Father sat beside him, talking to him calmly. Father had only his pants and jacket on, because both his shirt and undershirt were soaking in the copper kettle.

The cleaning-up operation took a good deal of time. Only after the floor, the sofa, and Father had been cleaned up and the cottage aired out did Jon begin to realize that he was exhausted, that his knees were shaking, and that everything around him was becoming more and more dreamlike.

He sat down on a chair by the window, where the blossoming heather was—it was flaming red in the dim light. Per-Anders' squinty eyes were fastened on him. The old man couldn't have anything to drink, but now and then Father moistened his lips with a damp cloth. A little while after that Per-Anders closed his mouth and began to look almost cheerful. His moans had stopped.

"If I just lie still . . . don't move . . . I don't have so much pain . . ." he managed to say with much effort. But he continued to stare without ceasing at the worn-out Jon.

"These are fine boys you have!"

Father looked pleased. The patient was talking coherently.

"Only one of them is mine—the one sitting over there."

"You could loan one of them to me. I am very lonely here. Yes, yes, I am. You have no idea how alone I am here!"

Per-Anders wrinkled up his face. His beard trembled. This was a far cry from the cocky old man Jon had remembered from the stall in Soltuna's open market.

"I understand," Father said in a half voice. "You really mustn't talk now, Per-Anders, but I understand. And you mustn't worry. Tonight you won't be alone at all. I had in mind leaving both of the boys with you."

The beard trembled even more than before. Father had cleaned the patient's face, and it looked pale and white but much better. Suddenly, two tears started to roll down his cheeks.

Rickard had come shuffling in in his worn-out wool socks. He stood by one end of the sofa smoothing out the blanket they had put over the old man's legs.

Father observed him carefully and seriously.

Astonished, Jon said, "Are we going to stay here? Both Rickard and I? But what about school tomorrow? How about that?"

"I'll call up the school and say that you are absent with my permission," Father said, stretching out his long legs. "There will have to be two of you here to help out, so that one of you can row over to Uddesund with a message in case anything happens and one of you can stay with Per-Anders. There's no doubt about it, and we really don't need to discuss it.

"Yes, Per-Anders, they are wonderful boys, and I think it's safer to leave them with you than to send for the dairyman's wife. For that matter, she couldn't get away because she has a new baby to take care of. And you can just take it easy; nothing's going to happen, but you're going to have a good bit of pain, and there's no doubt that tonight will be a bad night. I'll give the boys careful instructions. And tomorrow morning, I promise to come back. The bandages have to be changed. I'll rearrange my appointments. You know"—and here Father pointed his black beard at the ceiling of the cottage—"you know, I'm pretty proud of having been a surgeon again, and I think in time that I'll parade you around to the doctors at the hospital and say: 'Look here, this is the kind of job you can do with an old patient and two helpers!' . . . Yes, Rickard, what was it you wanted to say?"

"I noticed," Rickard said as he returned from the kitchen,

"I noticed that he has some pork and potatoes and eggs, and then there's some bread. Very fresh. Rye bread. Doctor, do you think . . ."

"I certainly *do* think so! When did we eat last? It was at least six hours ago. Oh, my! Fresh bread! That serves me right for complaining about the dairyman's wife. I'm sure she brought it. But call me Uncle Olof, Rickard, not Doctor."

Rickard gazed at the floor, shifting from one foot to the other. He continued in this manner as if he had to weigh everything before he spoke.

"And what about the chickens? I was thinking about them . . . they have to be fed and shut in for the night. Pretty soon it will be pitch dark!"

Per-Anders suddenly let out a cry. He had moved one of his legs. Father leaned over him.

"Best to lie still. Don't be worried. We'll look after the chickens. Don't you realize what sensible helpers we have here? I must say, I would have forgotten about the chickens otherwise! Come over here closer, Rickard, and perhaps Per-Anders can whisper to you where the chicken feed is and what needs to be done."

Both Jon and Rickard listened carefully to what Per-Anders had to say about the chicken feed, potato peelings, and water and about the forty chickens to be counted and shut in for the night.

Father looked out the window; it was getting dark. The darkness was beginning to seep into the corners of the room, near the cupboard, over by the ceramic oven. There were dark patches on the rag rugs, just as there had been sunshine a while back. Reds and blues had become black. Only the whites and golds were still visible.

150

"There's a lantern on the dock, and you'd better take it with you, boys. Be careful of the flame. I'll light the kerosene lamps in here while you're outside. And then you can start preparing some food. I'm ravenous! Do you still have enough strength for all that?"

Their answer was in the form of a headlong rush to the door. Feed the chickens, stay on Kalv Island overnight, no school tomorrow—and when they did go back to school, what heroes they would be!

Father got to his feet. Striking a match, he screwed up the wick in the kerosene lamp that hung above the table. It had a round yellow shade, and the glass was a little sooty at the top. The flame, which at the beginning was blue and uncertain, finally caught and began to burn clearly and evenly. The golden light spread warmth and comfort. Father went over to the window and lighted the candles in the copper candlesticks.

"Lights are going on in thousands of cottages and houses all over Sweden," he mused. "And how wonderful it would be if the people assembled around them could feel secure, healthy, free from illness and pain! How wonderful, too, if no one had to face the winter alone, without anyone to keep him company, without anyone to talk to when the long winter nights keep the cottage people shut in."

Minutely, Father began to examine Per-Anders' wrinkled face. With a good deal of effort, they had managed to change the sheet under him, and his head was now resting on a small pillow with a clean white pillowcase on it. His head was to be kept fairly low.

The patient lay there, as comfortable as possible and as well cared for as a baby.

Gravely, Father put the last of the newly sterilized instruments back in the bag and closed the two locks.

"You're lying there and worrying about something!" he said, suddenly breaking the silence. "I'll bet I know just what you're thinking. Something like this: 'Right now you're taking care of me, washing me, answering my every need. You're going to have someone watching over me tonight . . . and the next night . . . and perhaps a few additional nights . . . until I'm well again. But then? How is it going to be after that? It's December, and then come the real winter months when you and the neighbors scarcely dare to go out, and finally the days get longer. But it's all so eternally slow, so terribly slow. And even the nice days are only a matter of anxiety and unrest for one who is alone watching the years pass.' Now you listen carefully!"

Father sat down on the stool by the bed, pulled it up closer, and took the old man's hand with its somewhat gnarled long, narrow fingers.

"It's going to take more than an operation to make you well. It's going to take more to make you feel secure and contented so that you can begin carving your figures again. I'm going to propose something you can think over after I leave. Something to keep your mind occupied during the long hours of the night, Per-Anders!

"One of the boys with me, as I mentioned, is my own son —a boy we've both needed and enjoyed, and certainly I'm not about to let go of him. But the other one—well, it's just dimly possible that he can be put on loan to you. I happen to know a good bit about him—as a matter of fact, I helped bring him into the world—and for that reason, I feel I have some responsibility for the boy.

"He comes from dreadful surroundings—a drunken father, a worn-out mother who doesn't care any more, and brothers who are in some pretty sticky trouble with the law. Just between us, Per-Anders, I have reason to believe that the officials will soon intercede and try to get him away from the environment that sooner or later might cause him to go under, just as his family has."

Father loosened his grip on Per-Anders' hand. Instead, he had somehow gotten in touch with the old man's eyes. They were bright with fever but interested.

"He's a good boy, and he has a head on his shoulders," Father went on. "He goes to a good school, and he could make it into the Latin School this fall with a little support and help. It's not beyond the realm of possibility that he might get a good job in the Vidinge sawmills. There's a real future there for young, energetic, educated people.

"The house where he lives now"—Father's eyes traveled around the walls of the room, fastened on the porcelain dogs, the workbench, the bookcases—"is probably the worst dump in Soltuna. Full of . . . well, full of all sorts of things a boy shouldn't see and experience.

"It wasn't just a coincidence that I brought him with us today. To him, the country and a cottage like this are paradise. And the question now is: Doesn't Old Saint Per—in other words, you—hold the keys to the pearly gates?

"Something could certainly be arranged about his schooling. Probably he could ride in every day with the dairyman at Uddesund and ride back with him after he closes his stall at the market. He's a strong, muscular boy, and rowing across the cove would be no problem at all; I'm sure there are many youngsters around this area who have much more difficulty getting to school.

"When a person gets old, Per-Anders, there's only one thing better than to have someone around to help you—and that is to be able to help someone who really needs it."

Father saw a slightly worried look cross Per-Anders' face. Had he demanded too much of the patient, weak as he was? Had he miscalculated Per-Anders' reactions?

"Don't say anything now. As I said before, this is merely a suggestion for you to think over . . . at your leisure . . ."

But Per-Anders interrupted in a voice that suddenly seemed to have regained a measure of strength.

"What's his name—the boy you're speaking of? What should I call him?"

"Rickard," Father replied. "Rickard Svensson. But now, just hold still; I'm going to take your pulse. Give me your wrist! I'm pretty sure I heard them out on the porch, our boys!"

Rickard and Jon noticed the light of the kerosene lamp as they climbed up the hill. Their nostrils still retained the strange smell of the chicken coop. They had created quite a commotion down there when they appeared with the feed and filled the water trough that had been empty for so long. Eager bills pecking away, flapping wings, bobbing roosters' combs—neither of the boys had imagined that a few chickens could make such a lively fuss. They were there longer than they had counted on, because they felt responsible for seeing that even the tiniest and weakest among them—

the ones who seemed frightened and jumpy—got their fair share along with the more aggressive ones.

When they came out once again onto the hillside, after all the noise and commotion in the chicken coop, Rickard was carrying the lantern in his hand. And suddenly it was as if they were in a cathedral. Both of them turned their heads upward and gazed at the sky, alive with thousands of bright, twinkling stars—a brittle sight but a hopeful one, too.

Above the bay hovered a greenish half twilight, but the forest around them was dark. The woods on the far shore were like a protective guard keeping watch over the cottages and gardens.

Jon said, "I've been thinking about something. All he has, poor old Per-Anders, in the way of company are those chickens. Apart from them, he's completely alone. Not even a dog or a cat. You know, I think I'm going to ask Father if he doesn't think that one of Pixie's puppies should come out here to live. I had thought of asking the patron at Vidinge, but it would be better off here. More like a real home. Wouldn't that puppy have a great time here?"

As usual, Rickard thought the matter over before he replied.

"Lucky dog!" he said, once more turning his eyes toward the ground. "Lucky dog! What I wouldn't give to move in with it!"